The Talons of Iron Eyes

In pursuit of Squirrel Sally on his way back from Fort Liberty, the infamous Iron Eyes is bushwhacked by a pair of horse thieves who steal his thoroughbred palomino stallion.

Leaving him for dead, the outlaws head on to the logging town of Bear Creek. What neither man knows is that Squirrel Sally has observed the outlaws leaving the valuable palomino stallion at the livery stable. The fiery female realizes that Iron Eyes would never willingly part with his prized horse, and fears the worst.

Squirrel Sally sets out to find her beloved Iron Eyes and learn the truth.

By the same author

Iron Eyes
The Avenging Angel
Spurs of the Spectre
The Fury of Iron Eyes
The Wrath of Iron Eyes
The Curse of Iron Eyes
The Spirit of Iron Eyes
The Ghost of Iron Eyes
Iron Eyes Must Die
The Blood of Iron Eyes
The Revenge of Iron Eyes
Iron Eyes Makes War
Iron Eyes is Dead
The Skull of Iron Eyes
The Shadow of Iron Eyes
The Venom of Iron Eyes
Iron Eyes the Fearless
The Scars of Iron Eyes
A Rope for Iron Eyes
The Hunt for Iron Eyes
My Name is Iron Eyes
The Tomb of Iron Eyes
The Gun Master
A Noose for Iron Eyes
Fortress Iron Eyes
The Scalp of Iron Eyes
100 Golden Eagles for Iron Eyes
Iron Eyes Unchained
Iron Eyes the Spectre
Beware the Guns of Iron Eyes
Trooper Iron Eyes

The Talons of Iron Eyes

Rory Black

A Black Horse Western

ROBERT HALE

© Rory Black 2020
First published in Great Britain in 2020

ISBN 978-0-7198-3134-8

The Crowood Press
The Stable Block
Crowood Lane
Ramsbury
Marlborough
Wiltshire SN8 2HR

www.bhwesterns.com

Robert Hale is an imprint
of The Crowood Press

The right of Rory Black to be identified as
author of this work has been asserted by him
in accordance with the Copyright, Designs
and Patents Act 1988

*Dedicated with love and gratitude to my daughter Suzi and
granddaughter Alexia*

ONE

The moon was large and hung over the vast forested terrain in a fashion that seemed unearthly. The bright amber illumination cast down its light across the frosted trail the lone horseman was following. Yet the lone rider saw none of the brilliant scene from atop his high-withered palomino stallion as the sturdy mount continued along the crude trail that wound its way through the rocky area and a million tall trees. For unlike most horsemen who dared navigate their way across the Wild West, this intrepid pair of horse and master never stopped to make camp on their continuous journey.

The horseman did not trust the wilderness that he trawled in his relentless search for wanted outlaws. There were countless dangers hidden in the most innocent looking of terrains. The gaunt horseman was aware of all of them, and unwilling to risk encountering any of them. His early days had been different: then he had no choice. Nowadays he would sleep propped in his ornate Mexican saddle as the powerful stallion kept forging ahead in obedience to its master's sharp spurs.

Even asleep, the painfully lean rider would instinctively rock his long legs back and forth so that his spurs constantly touched the golden flanks of the thoroughbred animal, keeping it moving forwards. Yet if anyone ever observed the strange slumbering rider as he passed them on his journey they would have sworn on a stack of bibles that the hideously scarred face was wide awake.

The sleeping rider had a lifetime of brutal battles etched into his disfigured face. His once perfect features had been transformed into a patchwork quilt of scars. Most of his injuries had been crudely sewn up in the heat of battle by the mysterious horseman himself, to stem the bleeding quickly. But with each fight his appearance had become more and more monstrous.

His eyes were no longer capable of blinking, or even closing, which gave his already savaged features the look of someone who never actually slept. This only added to his reputation as being the living ghost who was unwilling to die. His long black hair hung straight on his shoulders, moving in rhythm with the momentum of his gallant mount as the stallion continued to drive ever onwards. Even asleep the infamous bounty hunter looked far more dangerous than his contemporaries.

Perched in the saddle on the animal's muscular back, the unholy horseman looked more like a corpse than a living creature. He defied rational description as the palomino stallion carried him through the vast forested hillside. No other living rider could ever have looked the way Iron Eyes looked.

The forest had gone eerily silent as the ghostly horseman made his way through its majestic trees. Each and every wild animal within its moonlit boundaries sensed that the most lethal of hunters was making his way through their land. The acrid scent of the rider wafted through the countless trees and filled the nostrils of the watchful creatures, who sensed the danger this man oozed from every pore.

Iron Eyes' powerful mount kept forging ahead at a pace few other horses could have matched. The stallion seemed to be the only animal within the forest that was oblivious to the sickening scent of death and killing that encompassed the bounty hunter.

Death rode unseen on the shoulder of the brutalized rider as his mount negotiated its way along the rough trail. It had always done so, as if guiding the merciless hunter to his next kill. The stench of death lingered on the skeletal figure draped in a battered blood-stained trail coat. The gore of countless victims mingled with his own spilled blood, and sent out a silent warning to every other living creature within the vast forested hills.

The wild animals sensed the unspoken danger that this gaunt figure posed. They would not willingly move from their lairs until he had drifted past them. It was as though they had some divine knowledge of the slumbering stranger which echoed in their pounding hearts.

A lifetime of killing had a scent that could never be washed from the terrifying horseman. A stench which was the only warning that the devilish bounty hunter ever gave his chosen prey.

Iron Eyes was still nursing the untended wounds from his last encounter with those determined to kill him only hours before. Sleep was the only medication he had to help heal his injuries. He would make the most of every second of it.

Iron Eyes had determined long ago that no matter how serious his wounds were, death would never take him. There was no place even in Hell for the likes of the savage bounty hunter. Death was his constant companion, protector and friend. It rode on his shoulder like a ravenous vulture, guiding Iron Eyes to his prey in the knowledge that the horrifically maimed bounty hunter would provide more victims to be taken back into the bowels of Hell.

The sturdy mount slowed and then stopped, abruptly waking its master, who raised his head and looked around the moonlit area.

After his head cleared, Iron Eyes inhaled deeply and then swiftly studied the surrounding trees. The bright moonlight gave all the appearance of it being daytime, but the bounty hunter wasn't that easily fooled, even though he had only just woken up.

'You nearly made me fall off, you damn gluepot,' Iron Eyes growled at the stationary horse beneath him. He gripped the silver saddle horn, and then swung his leg over the saddle's silver-encrusted cantle.

He heard the frosty ground crackle under his mule-eared boot as it returned to earth.

Without uttering a word, Iron Eyes took one of his numerous canteens from his saddle horn and removed its stopper. The palomino stallion watched as the pitifully lean figure snatched off his hat and dropped it on the ground before its hoofs. Iron Eyes filled the hat bowl with the precious liquid, and then carefully secured its stopper and returned the canteen to the saddle horn.

As the magnificent stallion drank the water from the hat, Iron Eyes silently reached back and flipped up the satchel flap of his saddlebag. His bony hand withdrew one of the numerous bottles of whiskey from within the leather bag, and raised its neck to his small sharp teeth. He extracted the cork from the bottle and spat it at the surrounding brush. He could survive for days and even longer without food as long as he had a plentiful supply of whiskey and cigars.

As the stallion continued to fill the silent area with the noise of its drinking, the skeletal bounty hunter put the bottle to his scarred lips and started to drink. The hard amber liquor burned its way down into his guts and cleared his head. Iron Eyes lowered the empty glass vessel and then tossed it between the trees. He dried his mouth along the sleeve of his battle-worn coat and sighed heavily.

The feeling of heat as the whiskey burned a route down into his innards helped the weary horseman. It kept the frosty air at bay – though it would never impair his judgement. For some reason, Iron Eyes had always been immune to the effects of any kind of hard liquor.

He slid one of the fresh batch of long slim cigars from the inside breast pocket of his trail coat and placed it between his teeth. His long fingers located a match and he struck it with his sharp thumbnail, then dragged its flame into the long black weed until his lungs were filled with smoke.

There was no sign of the stagecoach that the bounty hunter wanted to catch. The area was quiet. Too damn quiet. Iron Eyes briefly glanced back at the trail behind the hoofs of his muscular mount. He could just make out Fort Liberty in the distance, and exhaled a line of grey smoke at the sight.

'You covered a lot of ground, horse,' he said, before drawing smoke into his lungs and then expelling it. 'But you ain't caught up to that cantankerous Squirrel.'

The palomino raised its head and snorted. Droplets of water dripped from the animal's chin as its master plucked the hat off the ground and hung its drawstring against the gathering of canteens.

Iron Eyes' unblinking eyes darted around the scene like the honed killer he had become over the years, and he sucked on the thin black cigar. Smoke drifted from the teeth of the bounty hunter as he took hold of the long stirrup leather and grabbed his saddle horn again. He poked a boot into the stirrup and lifted himself back up into his saddle.

The moonlight caused the surrounding trees and undergrowth to sparkle as it fell upon the frosty vegetation. To most men it might have appeared unnerving, but not to the gaunt bounty hunter as he steadied the stallion.

As Iron Eyes gathered up his reins, his keen senses made him look all around the large horse. But the only sound was the palomino's snorting. The massive forest was as quiet as a graveyard.

That suited the bounty hunter. He liked graveyards.

Iron Eyes puffed on the cigar until ash dropped on to his hands. The large moon was so bright it allowed his narrowed eyes to see the countless tree tops that filled every square inch of land between where the powerful stallion stood, to where he had set out from.

He squinted hard at the distant fortress and then looked at the trail ahead of him. The trail wound its way through the trees like a snake in search of something fresh to sink its fangs into.

Then he recalled why he was here in the middle of nowhere.

After returning to Fort Liberty after rescuing the daughters of an old provision trader, in the course of which rescue he had been injured, Iron Eyes had been informed that Squirrel Sally had been at the fort while he was leading the rescue party, a small group of misfits, into Indian territory. But the feisty female had left the fort and returned to civilization before Iron Eyes got back.

Even though he was injured, Iron Eyes had set out after the young female. He reasoned that his powerful mount could catch up with her six-horse stagecoach. Yet as he chewed on the cigar, one thought kept gnawing at him. Why had Sally decided to leave the man she was besotted with, and head back to the relative sanctuary of the last settlement on the trail road?

This was not like the girl he called Squirrel.

She was too stubborn to run away, he thought. Squirrel was always up for a fight, and had killed quite a number of folks beside him over the previous year or so. In fact she had become quite a thorn in his side since he had first met her, and no matter how many times he had tried to shake her off, she kept after him. He still could not fathom why.

She had claimed that they were as good as hitched, and nothing could alter her mind. Squirrel Sally told everyone, including Iron Eyes himself, that he was her betrothed.

After tracking him to the remote Fort Liberty, had she simply turned her team of horses around and driven her stagecoach away? It made no sense to the hardened bounty hunter.

He had to discover why.

Iron Eyes swung the palomino stallion around and drove his spurs into its sides. The horse burst into action and cantered along the trail road. With every stride of the animal's long legs, the question kept nagging at the bounty hunter: why had Squirrel Sally left the fort?

No matter how many times he asked himself that simple question, he could not find an answer. His unblinking eyes tightened as they stared ahead at the moonlit trail. He thought about Squirrel Sally as cigar smoke drifted from his teeth.

Iron Eyes was becoming angry. He hated puzzles, and this was one hell of a puzzle.

He rammed his spurs into the flanks of the handsome palomino, and continued his wild ride after the tempestuous young female. The merciless bounty hunter had no idea why he was tracking Sally with such urgency – yet he was. He held the long reins firmly as the mighty stallion ate up the ground beneath its hoofs.

Iron Eyes did not know it, but he was acting exactly as Squirrel Sally wanted him to act: for once, he was blindly chasing *her* dust, instead of it being the other way around.

The golden stallion raced through the haunting light in answer to its master's spurring. Yet no matter how fast the handsome palomino went, Iron Eyes wanted the animal to find even more pace and go faster.

As the muscular stallion thundered along the moonlit trail Iron Eyes had no idea of the dangers that lay ahead in the depths of the forest. The skeletal horseman spat his cigar at the dust his mount kicked up, and gritted his teeth.

Squirrel Sally was somewhere ahead, and he was determined to find her. Nothing else would satisfy his burning curiosity and quench his thirst for answers.

TWO

The lantern-lit town of Bear Creek nestled in an alcove carved by nature out of the granite edge of the forest. Its numerous oil lamps glowed like fireflies against the ominous backdrop of tall black trees. A solitary trail road had been cleared out of the tree-covered hills by loggers as they made their way toward the remote Fort Liberty. Constant attacks by various bands of Indians had put an end to logging close to the edge of what had become known as the Indians' last stronghold. The wars that still raged beyond the fortress had claimed countless lives on both sides, and forced the loggers to abandon their plans to venture any further west. They now felled trees closer to Bear Creek, which offered them relative safety. Only the army and supply wagons now used the trail, which remained like a scar on the landscape to and from Fort Liberty.

The Indian wars had seen a vast reduction in the native population that had once dominated this remote land, but they were still a mighty force, as Iron Eyes and his small band of troopers had discovered to their cost only hours earlier.

Apart from the military travelling the trail, which snaked its way like a sidewinder through the dense forest, few civilians ever ventured this close to the hostile Indian lands. But the settlement of Bear Creek still thrived, as there was enough distance between it and the hostilities. Mostly loggers and storekeepers filled its five streets, regularly transporting its lumber to the rest of the ever-expanding states and territories. A few saloons dominated the main street, and supplied more than just hard liquor to its patrons: dozens of females in colourful dresses supplied something a little more personal and intimate to the well-paid loggers.

Music wafted on a cloud of stale perfume and tobacco smoke from the doors of the saloons, and filled the streets of Bear Creek. The sound of tinny pianos was like an unseen heartbeat, which promised even the ugliest of tree fellers a brief taste of paradise.

Then for more than a few minutes a strange noise came ringing out from the misty trail road. The sound of pounding hoofs and rattling chains resounded off the stout trees. To the superstitious it might have appeared that the spirits were heading toward Bear Creek.

Yet his was no supernatural force: this was real.

The six sturdy horses emerged from the gloomy mist of the forest and pulled the stagecoach into the bright moonlight and down a dusty slope towards the first of Bear Creek's numerous wooden structures. Within a few strides the team had entered the streets of the remote logging town as their unlikely mistress sat upon her high driving board and chewed on the stem of her corn-cob pipe.

The golden hair of the dust-caked female floated over her small shoulders and beat up and down like the flapping of an eagle's wings. Her petite body belied the fact that she was far stronger than her appearance indicated.

Sally Cooke's blue eyes sparkled in the street lantern light as she studied the surrounding structures far more carefully than she had when she had entered the dark forest in search of her beloved Iron Eyes. There were muscular men everywhere in various stages of drunkenness, and she expertly guided her team between them as the sound of pianos grew stronger.

Sally raised her ripped pants off the driver's board and started to press down on the brake pole with a bare foot. She had not paid any attention to Bear Creek as she had driven through it previously, but now her attention was as sharp as a straight razor.

To the sound of snorting horses and rattling chains, the long vehicle slowed almost to a walk as the horses obeyed the long reins being pulled back by the feisty female.

As the stagecoach started to pass the accumulation of open-doored saloons, Sally turned her head and looked through her long golden hair at the noisy structures. She pulled back on the reins and pushed her bare foot down on the brake pole. The coach slowly ground to a halt. As the vehicle rocked, Sally looped the long reins around the pole and pulled the pipe from her mouth.

Curiosity made her young eyes stare down from her high perch and into the saloon. Her small hands lifted her half-empty whiskey bottle from the driver's box, and pulled its cork. She took a warming swig from the neck of the bottle, then returned it underneath the seat.

The hard liquor burned a trail through the dust and flies that had accumulated in her mouth, enabling her to swallow them.

Squirrel had never seen such a gathering of large menfolk before, and it intrigued her young mind. So far she had not seen anyone less than six feet tall, and that fascinated her. It did not occur to the tiny female that this was a community of men who had to be bigger than most in order to hunk felled trees around.

A gravelly voice broke through her concentration as it asked her: 'What you doing, little girl?'

She swung her butt around on the seat and caught sight of yet another large man making his way towards the saloon. He touched his woolly hat and gave a nod in her direction. Her expression did not alter one bit.

Squirrel Sally did not answer as the logger passed beneath the stagecoach's driver's seat and laughed his way into the Diamond Pin saloon.

She watched as the saloon's doors rocked on their hinges as the logger made his way into the aromatic smoke. Her honed instinct could hear the raised voices of folks refusing to succumb to their weariness and leave the still busy drinking hole.

'These folks are plumb loco,' she muttered quietly. 'It's been dark for hours, but these varmints don't look like they're tuckered.'

Bear Creek seemed peaceful enough, but the spirited youngster still did not trust any of its inhabitants. Travelling with Iron Eyes had taught her that simple rule.

Sally reached down and plucked her trusty Winchester from the spacious driver's box before cranking its handguard and sending a spent bullet casing flying over her shoulder. She noticed from the corner of her eye, through her strands of golden hair, that other burly men were staring at her. They were standing near her two lead horses.

Squirrel Sally wondered why they were grinning in her direction. Perhaps it was the fact that she was an attractive young female which gained her their attention. She noticed other men looking at her as they wandered from one saloon to another.

Maybe it was the simple fact that she was sitting high above them, where most men did not expect an attractive young female to be perched. None of the loggers had ever witnessed a female in such a masculine position, and it both startled and amused them.

Whatever the reason for their mutual interest, it troubled Sally as she took another swig from her whiskey bottle. Her narrowed eyes watched the men slithering around in the moonlight and suddenly she felt vulnerable. Squirrel knew that men, especially big men, could pose a lot of problems for girls of a

18

certain age, and by the way they looked at her, she figured that she might have reached that age.

She fearlessly glanced at each and every one of the grinning faces before swinging her left leg over the side of the driver's high perch and descending to the boardwalk. Her small hands gripped her cocked rifle firmly as she moved slowly along the team of lathered horses. Reaching the lead horse, she paused and looked around the area as her index finger stroked the rifle's trigger in anticipation of trouble. The pair of loggers who had been standing near her horses had wandered off at the sight of her Winchester.

A few other drunken men gave her tiny frame a wide berth as they noticed her nervous right hand moulded around the Winchester's trigger.

She grinned to herself.

Even though the small female looked very feminine, it was obvious that she was probably the most dangerous person in Bear Creek. Unlike the majority of young women, the near-naked Squirrel Sally in her torn and tattered trail gear, silently warned everyone to keep their distance.

This was a tigress in human form.

Squirrel carefully checked the team of horses and then moved back towards the saloon's swing doors. The petite youngster stood on bare-footed tip-toes and was just about tall enough to look over the top of the swing doors.

The interior intrigued Sally as she watched the men and women moving around the sawdust-covered floor. The scent drifted out of the Diamond Pin

19

towards the body of the stage behind her narrow back.

Some of the bargirls were escorting men upstairs to the landing and a handful of rooms. Sally raised her eyebrows and wondered why. To her naïve mind, it made no sense, as the bar was where the whiskey and beer was.

She scratched her dusty chin and diverted her attention back to the heart of the saloon. Men were playing poker and keno at various tables as the rest of the feathered flock of soiled doves attempted to tempt them up the well-worn staircase.

Squirrel was puzzled. She counted eight females in differing stages of undress. They moved profession-ally from one table to the next in the most colour-ful of dresses. Unknown to the naïve Sally, they were still looking for fresh customers to bed and to relieve them of their last few dollars.

The scene was quite alien to the youngster.

She did not understand what she was observing. To her young mind, it simply did not make any sense. Sally had yet to understand her own maturing emo-tions, let alone those of average folks. She stared at the bargirls as they floated between the card tables in search of their final trick of the long night, and slowly shook her head.

'Them critters are just damn pitiful,' she sighed heavily, before being startled by a voice that came from over her shoulder. The voice was deep, and Sally felt every word as it touched her naked flesh.

'What you looking at, young lady?' It asked her.

Most folks would have jumped out of their skin, but not the defiant female. She was made of tougher stuff and considered the question. She tilted her head and raised an eyebrow, and looked at the tall figure behind her. This was the first sober man she had seen since arriving in Bear Creek.

'I ain't too sure, friend,' she admitted as her eyes surveyed the tall figure and spotted the glint of a tin star secreted under his top coat. Fearlessly she reached out and pulled the coat away from the star and nodded to herself. 'Are you a lawman?'

The question sounded as though she doubted that anyone who looked the way this man looked could ever be in such a tough profession.

'I sure am, Missy!' He grinned, and pushed back the brim of his hat before nodding at the beautiful female. He was about to take a step towards her, but felt the barrel of her Winchester stop his advance. His smile vanished as he looked down at the rifle.

'It ain't wise to poke a rifle into the guts of a sheriff, ma'am,' he drawled as he studied every inch of the tough youngster. 'You could get yourself arrested.'

Squirrel Sally returned the coy smile. 'Even a lawman can't arrest a varmint if he's dead. Back off, or you'll find out that I'm right.'

The sheriff eased himself away from the rifle barrel and looked her up and down. She was the most attractive female in Bear Creek beneath the grime and trail dust.

'But I ain't dead, little lady,' he said. 'And I've no intention of being dead any time soon.'

'You would be if'n you tried to jail me,' Sally informed him confidently. 'I don't like being penned in like an animal. It makes me kinda ornery. I'm plumb dangerous when I'm ornery.'

There was an element of wisdom and truth in her words. Her voice seemed to have a score of various accents mixed up together, and that intrigued the lawman.

'That I truly believe,' the sheriff stated. 'Who are you, anyway? I don't recall seeing you around these parts before. What's your name?'

'They call me Squirrel,' she sighed as she kept the firearm aimed at the lawman's innards. 'Leastways, that's what my betrothed calls me. I never stopped here before. I drove my team right through this little town on my way after Iron Eyes.'

The sheriff had heard the name of the legendary bounty hunter many times from a lot of folks. He doubted that even the man whom some regarded as a living ghost would ever tie himself down with a female, but looking at Sally, he could see why even Iron Eyes might be tempted.

'Iron Eyes?' the lawman repeated the name and stroked his clean-shaven jaw. 'Is he your betrothed?'

Sally raised her eyebrows until they vanished beneath her unkempt fringe. Her head tilted as she screwed up her eyes and glared menacingly at the sheriff.

'Of course he is,' she snapped. 'You don't think I trail any old varmint, do you? I ain't that kind'a gal.'

Casey Doyle had met a lot of folks in his time as the sheriff of Bear Creek, but none that were as perplexing as this petite female. He was trying to work her out when she slapped his ribs with the long metal barrel of her rifle and strode passed him towards her horses.

After exclaiming at this sharp but painful indignity, Doyle turned around and looked at the small female as she marched towards two of the town's drunks. They had made the mistake of lingering too long at the noses of her lead horses, and she was riled.

'What you galoots doing?' Squirrel shouted at the pair of giggling giants as they patted the exhausted horses. 'Leave my horses alone before I fill you full of lead.'

One of the pair waved a finger at Sally.

'You shouldn't talk to your elders like that, Missy,' he teased as his chuckling companion nodded. 'Me and old Luke here will have to spank your hide until your butt is red raw.'

Sally frowned angrily.

'What did you say?' she snarled like a mountain cat with its tail on fire.

Both the drunken loggers burst into laughter and rocked back and forth as they clutched their big bellies.

'She sure is a little fireball, Luke,' one of the men cried in fits of hysterical amusement.

'You're right, Cliff. I reckon she thinks she can get the better of grown men.' The other logger added.

The sound of the Winchester being fired echoed around the sturdy wooden structures as Sally sent a bullet into the boardwalk at the loggers' feet. Splinters showered over the large men, but this did not dampen their gleeful laughter.

Sheriff Doyle stepped towards the female, but faster than the blink of an eye, Squirrel Sally thrust the wooden stock of her Winchester backwards and caught him low.

Real low.

The lawman buckled and staggered backwards clutching the denim just below his belt buckle. The sight only made the two loggers laugh even louder.

There was one thing it was unwise to do, and that was to underestimate Squirrel Sally's temper, and the loggers had done both. Their joyous amusement only added fuel to the fire that burned in the petite youngster.

Sally gritted her teeth and moved closer to the pair of tree-fellers. She jabbed her rifle barrel into one of their bellies and caught his lowering head with its stock. The sound of teeth breaking made the other logger stop and watch as his pal fell backwards on to the moonlit ground.

'You shouldn't have done that, Missy,' Luke said, as he stared at his unconscious workmate. 'Now I'm gonna have to paddle your rear and teach you a lesson. We warned you.'

'And I'm warning you, pecker-head,' she screamed.

Sheriff Doyle had only just raised his head and opened his eyes when the sight of the tiny female defiantly kicking the rotund logger between his legs made his own mouth fall open. The lawman winced in sympathy as he watched the fiery female demolish the heavily built logger.

Doyle straightened back up just as the large man fell atop his unconscious friend. The sheriff cleared his throat as Sally swung on her bare feet and moved back towards him. He stepped backwards as she reached the spilling lantern light of the Diamond Pin saloon and bent over to inspect her torn pants.

'Ah hell. Damn it all,' Sally protested. 'I've done ripped my pants again.'

The lawman looked down on the doubled-up female as her long golden mane brushed the board-walk. He had no idea how to handle the small creature before him. All he knew for certain was that it was far wiser to remain out of range.

Squirrel Sally straightened up. Her hair flew back and caught the light of the oil lanterns that cascaded illumination across the street. It shimmered like a golden fleece and was enough to tempt even ancient Greek Argonauts.

'Look!' Unashamedly Sally shouted, pulling the torn fabric away from her skin to expose her fleshy groin. 'Cheap store-bought pants just ain't worth the buying, Sheriff. Lucky for me I brought a few extra pairs with me. I bought them back in Waco.'

Before the sheriff could utter a word, a drunken man staggered through the swing doors of the Diamond Pin and glided passed Doyle to the side of the stagecoach. Filled with hard liquor the oblivious logger began to unbutton his rough britches to relieve himself against the vehicle's large rear wheel. The drunk gave out a thankful sigh as a golden fountain emerged from his unbuttoned pants and splashed against the stagecoach.

The sheriff gasped and was about to warn the care-free soul who was relieving himself when his attention was drawn back to the young female who was glaring in fury at the sight. Sally cranked her repeating rifle into readiness. She leaned to her right and looked around the stationary Doyle.

'Get out of the way, Sheriff,' she fumed. 'I got me some shooting to do.'

To Doyle's horror he watched as Sally raised her rifle to her shoulder and closed one eye as she aimed.

'What you doing?' Doyle squealed before he hastily got out of the way of the Winchester's long barrel. The lawman waved his hands frantically at the handsome young female. 'Put that weapon down before you hurt someone.'

Squirrel Sally looked along her gun sights.

'That's what I intend doing. I'm gonna shoot that varmint's pecker clean off, Sheriff,' she said from the corner of her mouth as her finger curled around her rifle trigger. 'Nobody pisses on my stagecoach. Me and Iron Eyes had to kill a lot of "Wanted" critters to buy it.'

Before the sheriff could respond, a blinding flash spewed from the rifle barrel. As the town echoed to the deafening noise the drunken logger felt his hat shot from his head. The large man turned and stared at Sally as she clutched her smoking rifle in her hands. Blood trickled down from his grazed scalp.

The man turned and ran.

Sally gave out a belly laugh and blew her mane of wavy hair off her amused face. She winked at the sheriff.

'Reckon my aim is slightly off!' She grinned.

The lawman tried to work out what to do next. His only job as the town's sheriff was to keep Bear Creek as peaceful as possible, but this was not an easy task when you were dealing with hard-drinking loggers who wanted nothing more than to have fun, get drunk, and bed as many of the town's females as possible.

Squirrel Sally was a totally different sort of problem.

She was a wildcat. She was like nothing he had ever had the misfortune of encountering before.

The lawman cleared his throat and spat at the ground, then returned his attention to the petite fireball, who appeared to live by a code that he had never encountered before.

'Stop that, young lady.' He said as firmly as he could.

Squirrel Sally did not understand the effect she had on menfolk, but it constantly amused her. She sidled up to Doyle and looked up into his twitching features. Beneath the caked trail dust that covered every part of her, she was attractive. She raised a finger and ran a busted fingernail along his firm jawline.

'Ain't you kinda young to be a sheriff, pretty boy?' she purred in a low seductive tone. She watched as her presence enveloped the tall man. His facial

27

twitching grew more noticeable as he inhaled the unmistakable scent of the young woman below him. He looked down at the smiling Sally and cleared his throat again.

'I'm old enough,' Doyle said. 'I'm just wondering how old you are.'

'Old enough, I guess,' she replied.

'But how old?' the lawman stammered.

'Old enough for what exactly?' Sally teased.

Casey Doyle looked skyward, swallowed hard and raised his hands to push her away from him. The trouble was, Squirrel was far shorter than any of the town's womenfolk that he was more used to brushing aside in the execution of his daily duties.

The fingers and palms of his hands did not connect with her shoulders. They met with the well-developed bosom beneath her tattered shirt, and as he pushed, both hands cupped around her supple breasts.

He instantly realized what he had accidently done.

Doyle's shocked expression contrasted with the grinning female who fluttered her eyelashes at him.

'Is you playing with my chests?' Sally asked, and watched the lawman take a backward step.

He raised a finger and pointed at her.

'I don't know who or what you are, little girl, but you are dangerous and nearly killed that drunk,' he stammered in a vain attempt to regain his rapidly evaporating authority.

Like a creeping ivy, the formidable female moved even closer to the blushing sheriff and attempted to entangle him in her youthful grip.

'I already told you that folks call me Squirrel,' Sally said as her eyelashes fluttered in the moonlight like those of a newly born lamb. 'Why'd you grab my chests? Not that I mind, but is that what peace officers do in these parts?'

Sheriff Doyle waved both clenched fists at the heavens, peeled her off him and then marched back towards his office. He was muttering with every step of his long legs.

Squirrel Sally adjusted her shirt until it somehow managed to cover her nubile form. A wry smile etched her face as she climbed back up to the stagecoach driver's seat.

The smile had turned to laughter by the time she had released the hefty reins from the brake pole and gathered them in her small hands. She could see a large wooden structure set at the far end of the main street, and slapped the reins down on the backs of the six horses.

'Get moving, horses,' she called down to her team. 'I'm gonna bed you down in that livery stable yonder.'

The stagecoach slowly made its way towards the livery stable as Doyle stepped up beneath the sheriff's office porch roof. The tall lawman glanced over his shoulder at the grinning female perched high on the well-sprung board as she passed.

He pushed his key into the door lock, gave it a twist and entered his office quickly enough to turn and gaze from his window at the embattled stagecoach as it noisily rattled towards the aromatic livery.

Doyle rested his hands on the window frame and sighed heavily at the unusual sight. Sally turned her head and looked straight back at the lofty lawman.

The sheriff turned on his heels and moved to a blackened coffee pot sitting on top of his stove. He lifted it, gave it a shake and then poured its contents into a tin mug. As its fumes filled the young lawman's nostrils he walked back to the window and watched as the long vehicle entered the livery stables.

'That little gal is mighty troubling,' he said to himself, before adding: 'She sure is pretty, though. Awful pretty.'

THREE

The winding trail grew darker as the tree canopies reached out from either side and interlocked above the intrepid horseman as he lashed the shoulders of his handsome mount and forged ever onwards towards the distant Bear Creek. There was a new day coming, but it had yet to arrive in the large forest. The palomino stallion obeyed its master's urgent commands as the bounty hunter attempted to put as much distance between Fort Liberty and himself.

Iron Eyes had already lost too much blood during his valiant battle with the Sioux warriors deep in Indian territory, and it was about all he could do to stay alert as the horse thundered along the dark road.

His unblinking eyes glanced upwards. The bright moonlight was incapable of penetrating the dense canopy of interlocking trees, and that was the way Iron Eyes liked it. For a good quarter mile, the ground was black.

The gaunt horseman had never liked bright illumination. It betrayed every living creature beneath it, and could turn hunters into the hunted.

Iron Eyes raised his bloody fingers and ran them through his mane of long matted hair. His thoughts drifted as he fought delirium with every beat of his pounding heart.

During his youth he had lived in a forest not unlike the one he found himself riding through now. The eerie light had always acted like a shield to him then: it was his protector, and always had been.

The palomino stallion started to slow beneath its hefty saddle as the weary horseman grew more and more fatigued. Iron Eyes slumped forwards and loosened his talon-like grip on his long reins. His eyes darted to both sides of the wide trail road in search of unseen enemies, but he didn't see any. The stallion slowed to a canter as it neared a sharp bend in the road.

Iron Eyes was hurting. The savage injuries he had suffered at the hands of the Sioux braves only hours earlier had gone untended when he had been informed that Squirrel Sally had been to the remote fortress, but had left as unexpectedly as she had arrived.

The ghostly bounty hunter drew back on his long reins and looped them around the ornate silver saddle horn as the powerful horse came to a snorting halt. Iron Eyes pulled both his Navy Colts from his pants belt and dropped them into his deep trail-coat pockets. He felt them weighing heavily against his long lean legs beside the loose bullets he always filled his coat pockets with.

'I should have stayed at Fort Liberty and rested up on a cot for a few hours, horse,' he rasped angrily. 'I must be loco, chasing that little vixen. Squirrel might be only a gal, but she's as wily as any grown woman.'

Iron Eyes realized that he had made a grave error in not accepting the hospitality of the fortress. He regretted that simple fact. His wounds tormented his already brutalized frame as he slowly descended from the mighty horse and rested against the hand-tooled saddle.

For the first time in living memory Iron Eyes desired nothing more than to sleep. The sensation troubled the skeletal figure as he lifted the flap of his saddlebags and pulled out another full bottle of whiskey. He was about to raise it to his razor sharp teeth and pull its cork when his hand started to shake as pain racked his body.

The bottle slipped from his grip and hit the ground hard.

The sound of shattering glass filled his ears. His eyes looked down at the fragments and the whiskey-stained boots, but there was no emotion in his scarred face.

The stallion turned its head and stared through its long creamy mane at the unsteady bounty hunter. It snorted and pawed at the road surface.

Iron Eyes turned his head and looked through his own mane of limp hair at the accusing animal. He pulled a cigar from a pocket and placed it between his teeth, then scratched a match along the fender of his saddle. He cupped the flame and filled his lungs with smoke, only then noticing the bloodstain on his shirt front.

'Damn, I'm bleeding again,' he grumbled as smoke drifted through his teeth. The hideous sight of the scarlet stain disappeared as the match blew out.

Iron Eyes moved to his canteens and hoisted one off the saddle horn. After dropping the hat before his mount's hoofs, he unscrewed its stopper and then emptied its entire contents into the upturned hat bowl. Half of the water missed the hat completely as the swaying bounty hunter dropped the canteen.

'I'm in a bad way, horse,' Iron Eyes drawled, before climbing back up on to the stallion's broad back again. The only sound to fill the woodland was that of the horse drinking what water remained in the hat. Iron Eyes looked at the trail ahead, but it was blurred.

His bony hands rubbed his eyes, but they refused to focus.

Instinct told him that he had better ride on. He knew that he needed to find a doctor fast. His trembling left hand reached back and pulled another whiskey bottle from his saddlebags, and he pulled its cork with his teeth. He spat the cork at the surrounding trees, and then ripped his shirt apart to expose his pitiful torso. He then poured the fiery liquor over his bloody body.

The whiskey burned like Hell itself. Iron Eyes gritted his teeth as pain tore through his raw wounds. Few men could have tolerated such pain, but the horrific bounty hunter was unlike other men.

Shakily he pulled the cigar from his scarred lips and exhaled a line of smoke at the ground. Then he tossed the empty bottle into the black undergrowth and returned the well chewed tobacco stick to his teeth.

His mind was filled with a choking fog. It refused to clear or ease up as he sat for a few moments and forced himself to concentrate on the trail before his drinking palomino stallion.

Iron Eyes pulled the cigar from his mouth again. As smoke drifted from his teeth, he tried to think, but clarity was unavailable to his confused mind. The only thought that kept him alert was that of the small female he was attempting to catch up with.

Squirrel Sally troubled the thin horseman, as she had done since the very first time he had encountered her. He kept focusing his thoughts on the golden-haired female he was following. Squirrel Sally was a bewildering puzzle, and the cocktail of mixed emotions she never failed to stir in him might be the one thing that would keep him alert enough to achieve his goal.

Without warning, the silence was broken. A flurry of arrows burst from the undergrowth and sped towards the unholy horseman as he sat astride the magnificent stallion. But the golden horse had detected movement in the undergrowth long before Iron Eyes became aware of the Sioux warriors' presence.

The snorting animal reared up on its hind legs as the deadly projectiles homed in on their target. It kicked its hoofs at the arrows and then dropped down on to the moonlit ground. The massive horse did not wait for the sharp spurs to tell it to bolt: it leapt forwards and was galloping before any of the arrows had even reached the spot where the dazed bounty hunter had been slumped upon his ornate saddle.

Once again darkness had acted as his shield.

The palomino was as cunning as its master, and used the half-light to its advantage. The shadows that dominated this stretch of the road had a thousand ways to confuse any onlooker and the palomino used every one of them.

Iron Eyes held one of the long reins in his bony grip as his other skeletal hand dragged one of his Navy Colts from his deep trail-coat pocket and started firing over his shoulder at his attackers.

More arrows hummed in the night air as the archers released another volley from their bows after the demonic horseman. The sound of the lethal arrows buzzed in the otherwise silent air as Iron Eyes blasted his sixgun in reply.

The pounding of the stallion's hoofs echoed off the black trees that flanked the shadowy trail as the muscular mount kept charging away from the certain death the arrows promised to deliver.

'I thought them damn Injuns had quit trying to kill me, hours back,' Iron Eyes hissed as he instinctively switched his empty six-shooter for its identical twin and started firing again at the native bowmen. 'Reckon I was wrong again!'

The massive palomino stallion kept pounding through the darkness as arrows flew past it and vanished into the dense undergrowth.

The weary rider screwed up his eyes and lifted his head as the palomino weaved its way between the shadows that peppered the ground in patterns of curious shapes and sizes. Iron Eyes raised himself off his saddle and glanced over his wide shoulder at the Sioux warriors. A sense of relief washed over his painful body as he noted that none of them had ponies and were unable to chase him. Even so, more arrows cut through the air and passed mere inches from him as he attempted to gather his wits.

His index finger squeezed his trigger and fired blindly at the hostile group of warriors. He had no idea whether his aim was on target or not as he sat back down on the back of his galloping mount.

Iron Eyes glanced ahead as even more arrows were unleashed from their bows. As they flashed passed his slumped torso he managed to focus on the trail road.

'Injuns,' he growled angrily before whipping the stallion's shoulders with the end of his long reins. 'I hate Injuns even more than I hate cowboys.'

The bounty hunter leaned down over the neck of the palomino as the powerful animal turned a corner and rode into bright moonlight again.

They were safe now, Iron Eyes thought. Not even Sioux bowmen can make their arrows turn corners in pursuit of their prey. He pulled back on his reins and slowed the stallion to a trot before studying the forest that flanked both him and his horse.

It was an eerie sight. The trees loomed straight and appeared black as the bounty hunter felt the pain of his injuries returning to his mutilated body. A lifetime of battles and untended wounds hurt like fury. Iron Eyes wondered how many more times he could fend off the Grim Reaper before he, too, fell victim to death itself.

He felt blood trickle down his scalp and make a path between the numerous scars that dominated his face. He raised a hand, and his long bony fingers located a graze on the top of his head. One of the Indians' arrows had come closer to its target than he had first figured.

Then another thought managed to penetrate his foggy mind and troubled him: what if there were more unseen Indians waiting to bushwhack him along the bright moonlit trail? He had barely managed to survive that last attack, and it had only been the darkness that had helped him to do so. Now, in the unforgiving light of the moon, he doubted if he would be so lucky again.

There was nowhere to hide, and he knew it. He was a sitting duck should anyone else start taking pot-shots at him. Iron Eyes was uneasy. Even half dead, he was still aware of how vulnerable he was. He leaned forward and patted the horse's neck thankfully. The intrepid bounty hunter knew that it was the Mexican thoroughbred that had saved his bacon once again by producing an unbelievable turn of speed.

His thin hands gripped the reins tightly.

As fatigue started once again to overwhelm the gaunt figure, Iron Eyes mustered every scrap of his resolve and jabbed his spurs into the flanks of the powerful horse. The stallion increased its pace and continued towards Bear Creek. The thought that danger might still be waiting for him in the thickly forested shadows was enough to keep the bounty hunter moving ever onward.

His unblinking eyes looked down at his pitifully thin body and his whiskey-soaked chest: the wound was festering, but no longer bleeding. The whiskey had burned the wound relatively clean.

Iron Eyes tried to recall how or when he had been wounded, but no matter how hard he concentrated, his weary mind could not find any answers. Whenever it was that he had been injured, it was sometime during his daring rescue of the trader's two daughters, when he had guided them safely back to Fort Liberty.

His eyes darted back and forth in search of any more potential bushwhackers as he peeled the spent cigar from his dry lips and tossed it aside before locating a replacement and ramming the long slim tobacco stick between his teeth.

Iron Eyes chewed on the cigar thoughtfully and reloaded both his Navy Colts with the loose ammunition from his deep trail coat pockets. As the stallion continued to eat up the ground beneath its pounding hoofs a sense of danger kept gnawing at his innards. The bounty hunter was well aware that he was in bad shape and in desperate need of locating a doctor as quickly as possible, but it was the moonlit trail road that kept dominating his thoughts.

Again his tired brain thought of the Sioux warriors behind him and the possibility that there might be others between here and Bear Creek. He tried to urge the stallion into finding increased speed, but every sudden movement hurt. Riding the high-withered palomino was a torture. It felt as though he had been kicked by a mule, but the gaunt horseman knew that no mule would have dared kick out at the man known as the living ghost.

Defying the pain that racked his every movement, Iron Eyes reached back and pulled a bottle from his saddlebags. This time he was not going to waste its precious contents by pouring it over the savage wound in his belly. He extracted its cork with his teeth and spat it at the moonlit ground. His sharp teeth had already mutilated the cigar and turned it to mangled tobacco leaf. His bony hand wiped the leaf off his mouth.

He then raised the bottle to his lips and feverishly poured the whiskey into his mouth. Iron Eyes was parched. He did not lower the glass vessel until the bottle was totally empty and the hard liquor had burned a path down into his gullet.

Iron Eyes felt the whiskey fumes in his head as they rose back up from his innards and cleared his confused mind. He gave a sigh and then threw the bottle at the trees. He heard it smashing far behind him and nodded to himself. He jabbed his spurs into the flanks of the stallion until the palomino fully unleashed its power.

'I knew you was holding back, horse,' he growled at the mighty stallion as it charged on. 'Get us to that logging town while I'm still in a good mood.'

The palomino tried to obey its master's commands, yet no matter how fast the golden horse went, it did not satisfy Iron Eyes. A dark mood enveloped the rider, unlike anything he had ever experienced before. It was as if dark memories had raised their faceless heads and were screaming into his mutilated head.

Iron Eyes was angry. He sensed that death was close. Closer than it had ever been, and there seemed to be nothing the notorious bounty hunter could do to stop it from dragging him off the horse's back and hauling his pitiful carcass down into the bowels of Hell.

Iron Eyes should have been scared, but that was an emotion he had never understood. He was not frightened by death, but furious that it should be so close. The events that had brought him to this place were not of his design, but he was helpless to escape them anyway.

'Run horse,' he growled through gritted teeth, and lashed the sides of his mount with the end of his long reins. 'Run faster than you have ever done before.'

The palomino stallion thundered on.

FOUR

There were many differing types of men in the wild territory where the Indian wars still raged, but the most active were those who made their dubious living by stealing horses by any means possible. The cavalry alone had lost hundreds of mounts during their encounters with various tribes as the war progressed. The scavengers who roamed the wastelands knew that it was a profitable business to be in, and would kill anyone who stood in their way of obtaining the profitable equines. They were a heartless breed who respected none of the unwritten laws that men west of the Pecos lived by. If the rightful owners of valuable horseflesh did not want to part with their trusty mounts, they were simply sent to meet their Maker.

Jeb Snider and Bren Mason were two of the most black-hearted horse thieves that had ever darkened this section of the vast tree-covered landscape. Both men had graduated to their current status by obtaining every horse they set eyes upon until they boasted openly at their wealth. Yet no matter how much money they obtained, it was never quite enough.

They simply could not quit their unwholesome activities. It had become a drug to which they were totally addicted, and which they relished in the same manner as gamblers, who can never turn their back on a new hand of stud poker.

The pair of wanted men had managed to evade the law as they moved from one state and territory to the next, where 'Wanted' posters with their images were invalid.

Most sane men would have steered clear of the Indian wars, yet this only lured both Snider and Mason into the vast territory. Their appetites had been wetted by the promise of untold numbers of loose or abandoned horses, and this trade had made them more money than anywhere else they had operated.

Yet Snider and Mason knew they were quickly running out of places where they could continue to ply their dubious trade and profit from it. But like all men who have found a profitable area they could exploit, neither of the outlaws was willing to retire whilst there was still easy money to be had.

Leaving their camp at dusk, and with more than fifty head of horses roped in a temporary corral deep in the forested hills, the horse thieves steered their mounts through the dense trees towards the moonlit trail road.

Two days had passed since they had spotted the magnificent stallion being ridden towards Fort Liberty, and they knew that the horseman would be returning at any time. They silently hoped they hadn't missed the shadowy rider, but knew that the odds favoured them.

They eased back on their reins close to the moonlit section of the trail road.

'You reckon that varmint ain't passed here already, Jeb?' Mason asked as he steadied his exhausted mount. 'He might be long gone by now.'

Snider gave a chuckle. 'He was headed to Fort Liberty, and that's a long way off, Bren. By my figuring he's either still there, or he's about due to ride past here anytime soon.'

'We should have stayed here when we spotted that big golden stallion,' Mason moaned. 'I think it was a mistake to head on back to the horses.'

Jeb Snider gave a wry grin. 'Look, Bren. There's only one trail to and from that big old fortress. It stands to reason that he couldn't have got there and back in the time we was away tending our stock.'

Reluctantly Mason nodded.

'Guess you're right. It just troubles me that we might lose that palomino for the sake of feeding and watering them glue-bags back yonder.' He sighed.

Snider knew that the older outlaw was right in a way. The magnificent palomino stallion was a prize that he did not want to lose, either. Just like Mason, he realized that the large thoroughbred was probably worth more than all the horses they had accumulated so far. Palominos were rare in this part of the world, and highly valued.

'Quit fretting, partner,' Snider drawled. 'I bet you a two-inch T-bone that big old horse will pass by this very spot real soon. When he does, we'll get him.'

They dismounted and tied their reins to a couple of trees in a well-rehearsed action they had done numerous times before. Both men removed their cutting ropes from their saddles and started to uncoil them as they thought about the palomino stallion again. Neither of them had ever set eyes upon such a horse in all their lives.

As soon as they had seen the stallion days earlier they had realized that it would fetch a king's ransom, and bring them more money than they could get for their entire herd of horses. It was like finding a gold nugget in an otherwise pile of grey rocks. Both Mason and Snider wanted that stallion so bad that it hurt. Yet neither man had paid any attention to the gaunt bounty hunter astride the handsome horse. All they knew for sure was that he had ridden toward the distant fortress and would have to return. There was no other trail to take unless you wanted to risk your scalp and continue on into the heart of Indian territory, which they mistakenly thought impossible. Fort Liberty was not a place to linger in.

They figured that as soon as the horseman arrived there, he would take the earliest opportunity to ride back to the relative safety of Bear Creek.

'Who do you reckon was riding that big horse, Bren?' Snider asked his partner. 'I never paid him no notice. All I could see was that mighty stallion.'

Mason shrugged. 'Me too. Whoever the critter was, he must be plumb loco heading into the heart of Injun territory. I sure hope that idiot don't get that horse hurt.'

They both nodded in agreement.

Had they realized that it was the infamous Iron Eyes who was riding the palomino they might have had second thoughts of getting their hands on the animal. But sometimes greed could sway even the most logical of minds.

Mason led the way through the trees towards the edge of the moonlit road, with Snider following. Both outlaws were blissfully unaware that it was the notorious bounty hunter's mount they were planning to steal.

Snider stood beside his partner on the edge of the forested trail and studied the trees opposite. He was mentally choosing which one he was going to use to secure the rope in his gloved hands. A cold shudder washed over the younger of the horse thieves.

'What's wrong, Jeb?' Mason asked, as he toyed skilfully with the long rope in his own hands.

'It's kinda quiet, ain't it?' Snider said.

'It sure is,' Mason agreed.

The forest was unusually silent for this time of night. They knew that it was close to sun-up, and yet the forest was deathly still. Not even the birds seemed to be singing, and that troubled both men.

It was unnerving.

'I can't understand it, Bren,' Snider told his partner. 'I ain't ever known the forest to be this quiet before. Kinda spooky. Not even the critters are making any sound.'

Mason nodded in agreement as he shrugged.

'Look on the bright side, Jeb,' he muttered, thinking about all the money the large palomino would bring them. 'The quieter it is, the easier it'll be to hear that big horse when it gets close.'

Snider laughed and rubbed his whiskered chin.

'When do you figure we should string this rope across the road, Bren?' he asked.

Mason glanced at his partner. 'I reckon you should rig the rope right now, Jeb,' he answered cupping his left ear with his free hand. 'Listen up. I can hear heavy hoofbeats coming. No ordinary saddle horse makes that much noise. It's gotta be that stallion. He's coming back this way.'

Without uttering another word, Snider uncoiled his rope and secured one end to a sturdy tree trunk. Holding the rope in a firm grip, the outlaw ran to the opposite side of the trail road and looped it around another tree trunk.

'Is this high enough?' he called out to Mason.

'Higher,' Mason replied as he uncoiled his own rope. 'We don't wanna hurt that horse, do we?'

Snider raised the rope until his partner nodded. He tightened the slack until the rope was virtually rigid, and then ran through the moonlight towards his partner.

As Snider reached Mason's side again he noticed that his partner was holding his own rope like a wrangler. Mason was an expert at roping all kinds of animal, and had proved that many times. The horse thief was staring into the moonlight at the trail road. His grip tightened on the rope.

'Are you sure he's coming, Bren?' Snider asked in a low whisper. 'Are you?'

'I'm sure, Jeb,' Mason tilted his head towards the sound, which echoed off the countless trees. A wry smile etched his devious face. 'He's getting closer, boy – he'll be here damn soon.'

Snider dragged his .45 from its holster to check that all six of the weapon's chambers were full of fresh bullets.

'You reckon this critter will take much killing, Bren?' he asked the calm Mason as the older man toyed with his cutting rope to create a lasso. 'That palomino must be worth a fortune, and folks tend to fight a lot harder when you try to steal something valuable from them.'

Mason snorted.

'Don't go fretting about that varmint, Jeb boy,' Mason said bluntly as he held the rope in his experienced grip. 'He'll die as easy as all the rest.'

The younger horse thief grinned as he moved through the shadows closer to his partner. He cocked the hammer of his revolver and looked into Mason's face.

'Do you recall that fella in Wichita?' Snider laughed as the memory filled his mind with amusement. 'The rope stretched across the trail took his head clean off when he rode through it. Man, that sure was funny.'

Mason glanced at his chuckling pal.

'I recall you kicking his head around like a damn fool, Jeb,' Mason drawled before returning his attention back to the road. 'We ain't got time to play around tonight. We gotta kill that varmint and steal his stallion fast.'

Snider shrugged as the smile evaporated from his face.

'Reckon you're right, Bren,' he sighed and reached up to test the taut rope with his gloved fingers. There was nothing he liked better than seeing innocent riders knocked clean off their mounts by unforgiving ropes.

Suddenly both men's attention was drawn to the moonlit trail as it curled around a mass of trees. The clear sound of a horse's hoofs beating on the rough ground grew louder. Eagerly, both the merciless ambushers stared at the moonlit trail as an unearthly shadow came into view. It was the shadow of a horse and its rider.

'He's almost here,' Mason growled.

'I'm ready, Bren!' Snider hissed like a sidewinder in anticipation of sinking its fangs into the flesh of its approaching prey. He gripped his .45 tightly and stroked its trigger. 'Soon that big horse is gonna have itself a couple of new masters.'

Mason nodded in agreement as he readied the uncoiled rope to lasso the valuable prize. The outlaw grinned cruelly. His wrist began to rotate the looped rope faster and faster until it sounded like a swarm of hornets.

FIVE

Both horse and rider were utterly unaware of the danger that awaited them around the long winding moonlit bend as they continued to gallop between the towering trees along the trail road. The massive palomino stallion had not slowed its brutal pace for more than ten minutes as its powerful legs ploughed up the dust beneath its pounding hoofs, carrying its injured cargo on toward Bear Creek.

Yet Iron Eyes had not noticed. His emaciated body was propped between the silver embellishments of his hand-tooled saddle like a child's rag doll. The severely injured bounty hunter had once again succumbed to the swirling whirlpool of unconsciousness and was drifting in and out of enforced sleep. Only his instinct for survival managed to defy his overwhelming need to fall off the cliff edge between life and death. Time and time again it dragged his pitiful being from the jaws of eternal slumber, as the gallant stallion continued to gallop through the eerily moonlit forest, and on towards the distant logging settlement.

Iron Eyes rocked on the high-withered palomino and every few moments managed to see the passing scenery. Yet he was unable to remain fully alert for more than a few moments as the desire to sleep overwhelmed his brutalized body: no matter how much he wanted to fall from the saddle and sleep for eternity, some unseen hand kept the haunting horseman firmly in place.

Years of practice ensured that the painfully scrawny bounty hunter remained in his saddle even when totally asleep. But to any onlooker the hideously maimed Iron Eyes appeared to be wide awake, his unblinking eyes staring blankly ahead at all times.

It was impossible to tell whether Iron Eyes was awake or asleep. His bullet-coloured eyeballs remained fixed ahead and dared anyone to take their chances. For decades, various tribes of Indians had claimed that Iron Eyes was not a living man at all. They believed that he was a spirit of utter evil – a man who could not be killed because he was already dead, but the Devil refused to allow him to enter the bowels of Hell. The hideous scars that dominated his once ordinary appearance now added fuel to the legend that he was actually a living corpse and too ornery to die.

Utterly unaware of the danger, the palomino powered around the bend in the trail and headed on towards the cutting rope that was stretched across the wide road. Had Iron Eyes been fully conscious he would have spotted the danger immediately, but the bounty hunter was far from conscious.

Both Mason and Snider looked on eagerly at the sight of the handsome palomino stallion as it came hurtling towards their potentially lethal trap. But the sight of the handsome horse was soon obliterated from their collective minds when they focused on its rider. Neither of the horse thieves had ever seen anything like the horseman who was steering his mount towards them.

They gulped in horror as the moonlight cast its eerie illumination on the mutilated face of Iron Eyes. It was like staring at death itself heading towards them at breakneck pace.

'Look at him,' Mason gasped in terrified disbelief.

'What the hell is that?' Snider gasped as he caught sight of the face bathed in the moonlight. 'That varmint ain't no normal critter, Bren. He's a monster! He's a damn monster!'

'Calm down, Jeb,' Mason urged his partner in crime as once again he started spinning his lasso feverishly. 'Just remember why we're here.'

Jeb Snider dried his sweating face with the back of his sleeve and nodded to the older man. It wasn't easy to ignore the sight of the spectre galloping straight towards them and the potentially lethal rope they had rigged in his path.

'You reckon that varmint will be as easy to kill as most folks?' he asked nervously. 'He don't look much like regular folks.'

Mason did not reply. There were no words that could describe the sight that the pair of merciless horse thieves were staring at from the shelter of the trees. A cold chill traced down the backbones of both secreted men as the stallion carried its master ever closer. The sound of its pounding hoofs echoed off the surrounding trees like the drums of Indians just before they made war.

For the first time in their lives, they were frightened.

The half-asleep Iron Eyes sat rigidly on his high-withered mount, staring blankly ahead with unseeing eyes. Yet the pair of treacherous onlookers had no inkling that their chosen prey was not seeing anything apart from the nightmarish dreams his feverish brain was mustering.

Iron Eyes' mane of long black hair beat on his wide shoulders like the wings of a vampire bat in search of sanctuary after filling its belly with the crimson gore it craved. Yet nothing could be further from the truth, as the skeletal bounty hunter was in desperate need of the precious blood he had already lost during the previous twenty-four hours. Few creatures could survive for long without enough blood in their body, but the gaunt horseman had defied death many times.

But for Mason and his companion it was still like watching the spectre of death approaching. Iron Eyes' pathetically ragged form rode through the shafts of moonlight that striated the trail road towards the outlaws.

Neither of the horse thieves had ever seen anything like the sight of the daunting bounty hunter as his horse closed the distance between itself and the taut cutting rope. Within a mere heartbeat the golden stallion had ridden safely beneath the rope – but its master was less fortunate.

No sooner did Iron Eyes feel the rope catch his blood-soaked chest than he was dragged from the saddle and his pitifully lean body hurtled through the air backwards. Like a helpless ragdoll, he crashed on to the trail-road surface and cartwheeled over and over for a further ten yards before coming to an abrupt halt. The back of his head collided with the unforgiving hard ground, and once more the bounty hunter felt himself drowning into an ocean of darkness.

Even before Iron Eyes had crashed into the ground, Bren Mason had lassoed the stallion and hauled it to a stop as his partner advanced towards the crumpled heap that was the famous Iron Eyes. The outlaw could not disguise his horror at the sight at his feet as he reached the motionless bounty hunter. He grimaced and pondered the stomach-churning sight, with his cocked .45 aimed at the bleeding body. As Mason led the captured stallion to his side, he too looked down in disbelief at the horrific sight.

Both outlaws stared down at the human wreckage. Blood had seeped from a fresh graze on Iron Eyes' scalp, and sent streams of crimson gore trailing down the scars on the maimed features.

Nothing they had ever witnessed before resembled the sight of the unblinking eyes staring blankly heavenwards as blood trailed down his face. It shocked both men.

'Reckon I'd better shoot this monster, Bren,' Snider said, and aimed his gun at the busted face and twisted body on the ground. 'We don't want him coming back to life.'

Mason shook his head. 'Don't bother, Jeb.'

Snider glanced at his partner.

'What?' he queried.

'He's dead,' Mason spat as the stallion fought with its captor and pulled against the cutting rope, which had perfectly encircled its head and neck. 'Any fool can see he's dead.'

Snider kicked at the crumpled body. Iron Eyes' right arm fell across his bloody chest in a fashion that showed no hint of life.

'The fall must have killed him,' he shrugged. 'Looks like he busted his neck.'

'Don't waste a bullet on that dead critter, Jeb,' Mason growled, then turned and tried to calm down the powerful stallion as it fought for its freedom. 'Go get your saddle rope off them trees and then bring our mounts here.'

Snider did as the older outlaw told him. He holstered his gun and ran to where the rope was secured before coiling it up and hanging it from his saddle horn. The horse thief was nervous as he led both their mounts to where Iron Eyes lay in a pool of his own blood where Mason waited.

'Are you sure he's dead, Bren?' Snider checked.

'Nothing living could look that bad, Jeb,' Mason confirmed.

Mason mounted his horse and tied the rope holding the palomino in check to his saddle horn. He rubbed his sweating face and stared at the massive stallion in its finery. The ornate saddle was covered in silver accessories and caught the first rays of the rising sun. They glinted like jewels and caused the outlaw to smile.

'Look at this saddle, Jeb boy,' Mason said.

Snider stepped into his stirrup and hauled himself on to his own mount. He looked at the expensive saddle and the finery that accompanied it, and nodded in agreement.

'That saddle must be worth a pretty penny, Bren,' he said.

Mason turned his head and looked down on the crumpled mess that was Iron Eyes and then tilted it back to stare at his partner again.

'The thing that's nagging at my craw is,' he began, 'how could a varmint that looked like him afford a fancy rig like that? And how could he own such a horse? These golden nags cost a fortune by all accounts. It just don't figure.'

The younger horseman steered his mount closer to Mason as the morning sun warmed their bones. Snider bit his lower lip and shook his head.

'You're right, it don't figure,' he agreed looking at the palomino stallion. 'That fella looks more like a scarecrow than anyone I've ever tangled with. How could he own such a piece of horseflesh like this 'un?'

Mason turned his mount. 'I'm through trying to figure this out, Jeb. Come on, it's time we got out of here.'

The saddle horses were made nervous by the presence of such a large thoroughbred horse. The animal was at least two hands taller and far sturdier.

'Where we headed, Bren?' Snider wondered as he watched his partner spur his horse, leading the valuable palomino behind him. The younger outlaw spurred his own horse and followed the handsome stallion.

Mason glanced over his wide shoulder.

'Firstly we're going to Bear Creek to rest up for a couple of days, and then we're taking this fine animal to Utah and selling it to the highest bidder.'

'Why Utah?' Snider asked.

'We ain't wanted in Utah, that's why!' Mason laughed.

They rode on towards Bear Creek at a pace that suited them both. The devilish men had gotten what they had set out to get, and it was time to celebrate.

As the saddle horses led the handsome stallion down a steep slope towards the remote settlement of Bear Creek, the limp arm of Iron Eyes slid off his chest on to the ground. As the rays of the sun warmed everything beneath its rising glory, the talon-like fingers of the hand twitched. Soon they started to claw at the dust.

Iron Eyes was not dead.

SIX

The morning sun had risen just enough to peak above the tops of the numerous cabins down the centre of Bear Creek as the pair of horse thieves emerged from the forest. A line of blinding sunlight spread up the main thoroughfare and on to the trail road cut between the numerous trees. Yet nobody seemed to pay the horse thieves any heed as they entered Bear Creek. Mason rode slightly ahead of his partner, leading the powerful palomino behind his own saddle horse. Snider kept a watchful eye on the awakening inhabitants as they slowly emerged from their homes and the various brothels. Even though it was only just after dawn, most of the burly men had already made their way to the various logging camps to start another hard day's work.

It had been more than an hour since they had left the twisted body of Iron Eyes on the trail road and departed for the logging settlement with their latest acquisition in tow. Mason chewed on what was left of his cigar, and finally spat its tormented remnant at the sandy street. Nervously he kept glancing back at the powerful stallion he had roped to his saddle horn. He was dog tired. The high-withered stallion had rebelled every step of the way after it had been unceremoniously taken from its notorious master by the outlaws. The golden horse was still bucking against the rope around its neck as Snider and Mason started down the centre of Bear Creek's main street.

'Ain't many folks up and about, Bren,' Snider said from the corner of his mouth as they cautiously passed the sheriff's small office. 'The town's darn quiet. Too quiet for my liking.'

'Mark my words. It'll get friskier as soon as nightfall returns, Jeb,' Mason said as he looked back at the wide-eyed palomino. 'I sure wish this damn horse would settle down for a few minutes and quit trying to break free.'

'I wonder who that critter was, back there,' Snider said thoughtfully. 'I never seen anyone that looked as bad as he did.'

'I figure he was a varmint in the same line of work as you and me, Jeb,' Mason rubbed the tobacco off his tongue and spat at the ground. 'It sure is strange how much this big horse didn't like being parted from him, though.'

'That is kinda odd,' Snider agreed with a shrug of his shoulders. 'Maybe this palomino got a soft spot for monsters, Bren.'

The older of the outlaws gave out a belly laugh that echoed off the log cabins. Mason slapped his leg and nodded.

'We killed his favourite monster,' he roared.

Snider raised an arm and pointed ahead to the end of the long street. 'There's the livery, Bren. Soon we can park the animal there and go get us some vittles.'

Mason nodded. 'I tell you something, Jeb boy,' he said as he leaned back and gripped the cutting rope that held the bucking horse in check. 'If this palomino wasn't worth so much, I'd have put a bullet through its skull by now. He almost ripped the saddle off my horse's back, and me with it.'

'Maybe he thinks we're taking him to the glue factory,' Snider grinned as they reached the large open barn doors of the livery stable and stopped their mounts. The reluctant palomino stallion still bucked and tugged at its restraints, and snorted as both the horse thieves dismounted and tried to calm it down.

But the stallion could not be calmed by either of the horse thieves. It rose up on to its hind legs and lashed out in fury with its hoofs at both Mason and Snider. After a while they backed away from the snorting animal.

'I'll be glad to see the back of this damn ornery critter, Jeb,' Mason admitted as he took refuge between their saddle horses as the golden horse continued to vent its wrath. 'He'd kill us if we gave him half a chance.'

'You're right,' Snider gulped in agreement. 'Beats me how something so pretty can be so damn loco.'

Their conversation came to an abrupt halt as the horse thieves heard a noise coming from within the livery behind their wide backs. The burly blacksmith walked out into the sun and stared curiously at the bucking palomino. The muscular man ran his large hands through his thinning hair as he observed both Mason and Snider.

Joe Carter had been around for too long to make the mistake of asking the two fully armed strangers how they happened to be in possession of such a valuable hunk of horseflesh, and why it was adorned in its finest livery. He knew that it was mighty dangerous to be too curious this far west of the famed Pecos river. Men tended to get ornery and start firing their guns if a blacksmith showed too much interest.

He moved around the dust-caked saddle horses and patted the golden stallion on the neck. For some strange reason, the palomino immediately calmed down as the powerful man walked around it until he was nose to nose with Mason.

'How'd you settle this horse down so easy?' the older of the outlaws asked the blacksmith.

Carter ignored the question as he stroked the nose of the exhausted palomino. It was a gift that few of his profession shared. He tilted his head and studied both men silently. It was not the horses' hoofs that frightened him: it was the guns that both the strangers sported which concerned him most.

'You wanna rent a few stalls, stranger?' Carter asked as he pulled out a lump of tobacco from his apron pocket and took a bite from its length. 'Reckon they horses need a rub down and oats while you rest up.'

Both outlaws nodded.

'Yeah, that's exactly right,' Mason piped up as his companion kept a beady eye on the sheriff's office down the street. 'We want three stalls for the nags. We've travelled a long way, and they're plumb tuckered out.'

Carter glanced along the road. He knew that Fort Liberty was the only hint of civilization along that dangerous trail but decided not to mention it.

'The horses are real lathered up,' he noted. 'Don't worry none. I'll wash them down before I feed them. Give them twenty-four hours and they'll be as good as new.'

Mason dipped his fingers into his vest pocket and pulled out a handful of silver dollars. He handed them to the blacksmith and touched the brim of his hat.

'Much obliged,' he rasped as Carter pocketed the money, took the reins of the saddle horses and started to lead them into the far cooler stable.

After the three horses disappeared from view, Snider moved closer to his companion and rubbed his whiskers.

'I'm real hungry, Bren,' he stated rubbing his guts.

'Me too,' the older outlaw said as he looked around the sturdy structures until he found what he was looking for. 'Look over yonder, Jeb. I see a place for eating.'

The alluring aroma of fresh baked bread and a warming stove filled the air. It was something the outlaws had missed during the previous month as they had gathered up the small herd of horses.

Mason and Snider strode away from the livery stable towards the delicious smell. Within less than twenty yards they reached their goal and stepped up on to the boardwalk. The hungry horse thieves eagerly entered the café.

Neither of the wanted men had considered that anyone in Bear Creek would notice their arrival, but one feisty female had done just that.

Propped on her knees, Squirrel Sally had been peacefully sleeping under a pile of hay when she heard the three men talking below the high stable loft's open window. The voices had abruptly awoken the young female from her deep sleep. Curiously she had crawled closer to the open loft window and stared down unobserved at them. Yet it was not the men who drew her interest, but the distinctive horse they had in tow.

Sally had heard the distinctive noise the powerful stallion made many times since she had been travelling with the legendary Iron Eyes. Maybe it was this sound that had awoken her, she surmised.

Just like people, no two horses were the same. As the three men talked, Sally had stared down from her high vantage place at the familiar palomino stallion, and silently gasped in bewilderment.

It seemed impossible that Iron Eyes' prized mount would be in the possession of the two men. But that was what she had seen. Sally was baffled. She rubbed her eyes, but the vision had remained the same.

The sound of the café door closing across the wide street seemed to spur Sally into action. She jumped to her feet, moved to the edge of the high parapet and looked down on the blacksmith and the three very different horses he had just led into the heart of the livery.

The longer Squirrel Sally looked, the more she was convinced that the powerful stallion was Iron Eyes' prized possession. No two palomino stallions could possibly be dressed in exactly the same fine livery as the golden horse belonging to her beloved bounty hunter, Sally silently told herself as her toes curled around the edge of the wooden parapet.

It was impossible, she thought. The Mexican saddle had been created by the finest artisans south of the border. How exactly Iron Eyes had managed to get his hands upon such an expensive horse and silver-encrusted saddle was unknown to the feisty female, but there was no mistaking it, either.

She was staring down at the notorious bounty hunter's most prized possession, and she knew it. The pair of rugged men she had just observed below the hay-loft window had somehow gotten their hands on something that her beloved Iron Eyes would not willingly give anyone.

A cold shiver washed over her.

Only a dead Iron Eyes would part with his magnificent stallion, she thought. Sally swallowed hard and blew her golden locks of hair off her attractive face.

Had his luck finally run out?

Could those men have bushwhacked Iron Eyes?

Had they somehow managed to kill her betrothed? They did not look capable of bettering the renowned bounty hunter, but looks could be deceptive.

Fury turned into anxiety as her heart pounded inside her petite torso. Her breasts heaved as she ran her fingers through her unkempt hair.

Iron Eyes could not be dead, she thought. He just could not be dead. Yet the more she considered the few facts she had at her disposal, the more likely it seemed.

Every sinew of her small body wanted to confront the rugged outlaws and kill them, but she knew that somewhere between Bear Creek and Fort Liberty Iron Eyes might be in urgent need of help.

Help that only she could deliver.

Sally picked up her trusty Winchester repeating rifle off the makeshift bed of hay, and then proceeded towards the top of the ladder that protruded a couple of feet above the floor of the loft. She grabbed the ladder and swung her curvaceous form off the edge of the platform and descended towards the floor of the livery.

As she reached the ground, Joe Carter turned his head and caught sight of the female. The look on her face was totally different from when she had arrived in the middle of night and left her stagecoach and team of six muscular horses in his expert care. For a silver dollar he had permitted the fiery female to sleep up in the stable loft.

Carter felt a bead of sweat trail down his crusty features as he studied her face. Squirrel Sally's innocence had been replaced by a hardened frown as she gripped her trusty rifle in her hands and glared at him.

The blacksmith moved away from the three horses that Mason and Snider had left in his care and towards the grim-faced vixen, and studied her. Few people had ever troubled the well-constructed Carter, but Squirrel Sally managed to unnerve him.

Without uttering a single word she cranked the rifle into readiness. A casing flew from the magazine of the Winchester and over her shoulder.

'What's wrong, little one?' Carter asked the advancing female as she closed the distance on him. 'You look mighty upset about something.'

Sally did not reply. She marched passed the blacksmith and did not stop until she reached the high-withered palomino stallion. Her worst fears were confirmed as she got a closer look at the unique leather carvings on the saddle fender. She recognized them.

Then Sally moved to the saddlebags and lifted the flap of the closest satchel and stood on her toes to dip her hand into it. Her worst fears were confirmed as she felt glass bottlenecks.

She pulled out a whiskey bottle and stared at it.

'Iron Eyes,' she uttered soulfully.

Carter cautiously moved between the dust-caked saddle horses to the larger palomino and the handsome female who held the whiskey bottle in one hand and the lethal Winchester in the other.

'What's wrong, Missy?' he repeated, as he watched her staring blankly at the bottle of hard liquor. 'Ain't you seen a bottle of whiskey before?'

The question was misguided and badly calculated.

Squirrel Sally stared up through the wavy strands of her golden mane at the blacksmith. Her expression altered as she swung her rifle up and pushed its metal barrel into Carter's throat.

'Do you know them varmints that left this horse with you, old timer?' she growled furiously as her finger stroked the rifle's trigger. 'Do you? Answer me, or I'll surely kill you.'

Carter shook his head as he felt the cold steel press into his Adam's apple. 'Nope, Missy. I never seen either of them galoots before.'

For what felt like an eternity to the blacksmith, the frowning female did nothing as she glared at him. Then as quickly as she had raised the Winchester, Sally lowered it. She nodded and pushed passed the muscular man.

Squirrel Sally inhaled loudly and then pointed the rifle at her stagecoach.

'Get my team hitched up to my stage, old timer,' she said in a low, ominous tone. 'I'm heading back to Fort Liberty.'

The big man nodded, and rushed to the individual stalls where all six of her stagecoach team were secured, and began obeying her orders as quickly as he could manage.

As Carter led each of the animals out from their stalls in turn and began readying them, he kept glancing over his muscular shoulder at the silent Sally. She appeared entranced by the bottle of amber liquor.

Squirrel Sally was staring thoughtfully at the whiskey bottle in her hand as she stood beside her battle-weary stagecoach. Whatever thoughts were filling her mind she was keeping them to herself. Then with the agility of a mountain goat, she climbed up the side of the stagecoach to the driver's box. She sat down and watched the large man doing as instructed.

Joe Carter continued to ready the horses and secure them to the traces. The sound of loose chains clattering as they were buckled to the harnesses filled the livery stable as the blacksmith worked feverishly to obey the rifle-toting female perched high above him.

The blacksmith was only too aware that Sally not only had a whiskey bottle in one small hand, she also had the deadly Winchester gripped firmly in the other. One by one, Carter began hitching the sturdy horses to the long wooden traces that were attached to the stationary stagecoach.

The blacksmith worked as fast as his lumbering frame would allow, for Squirrel Sally troubled him in the same way that she disturbed everyone who encountered her. Even the legendary Iron Eyes, who was known to be fearless when faced by his many foes, was always troubled by her. The famed bounty hunter did not understand any womenfolk, but Sally totally bewildered him.

Joe Carter was equally perplexed by the tiny female. Her beguiling beauty gave no hint of the volcanic emotion she harboured. She could explode like a barrel of black powder at any time, and often did.

Suddenly without warning, Sally looked down in his direction. She drew his attention with a whistle that blew her golden hair off her face.

The burly blacksmith paused and looked up at her. 'What?'

Sally gripped the lip of the driver's box with her toes and leaned forwards. Her blue eyes focused on Carter.

'Have you got a doctor in this town, old timer?' she unexpectedly asked. 'I figure I need a doctor.'

The blacksmith looked at her. 'Are you ailing, Missy?'

She threw her head back and gave out a belly laugh.

'There ain't nothing wrong with me,' Sally laughed before resuming her serious expression. 'Answer me. Is there a damn doctor in this town?'

'Yep,' Carter nodded in reply. 'Doc Parry has himself a cabin on the edge of town. You can't miss it. He has himself a brass shingle nailed to the door with his name on it. Why? Why you be asking about a doctor?'

The petite female nodded to herself as a plan formulated in her young mind. Normally she just followed Iron Eyes blindly and aided the gaunt bounty hunter in whatever he was doing, but now things were different.

She had no proof that Iron Eyes was hurt, or even worse, apart from the palomino stallion standing ten yards from her, but she sensed that if she did not act, her worst fears would become a reality. Every sinew in her shapely form knew that her beloved bounty hunter would never be parted from the stallion willingly, and that thought fermented in her.

'You OK, Missy?' Carter asked.

Sally did not respond. She placed the bottle down into the box at her bare feet.

With her rifle placed across her thighs, she watched Carter from her high perch like an eagle studying its prey on a warm thermal. As the plan continued to develop in her mind, Sally fumbled for her tobacco pouch, set down in the box with a collection of clay pipes. She began to fill the bowl of one of the pipes as she carefully watched the hard-working blacksmith.

'Keep working, old timer,' Sally said, as she struck a match and sucked its flickering flame down into the pipe bowl. As her lungs filled with smoke, she thought about the gaunt bounty hunter and pondered on what might have happened to him. Every fibre of her being sensed that time was running out.

Carter led the last two sorrels out of their stalls and backed them towards the other four horses. He could not understand what was happening, or why the handsome young vixen seemed so anxious. His large hands hooked the chains to the traces.

Smoke billowed from her mouth as the disturbing notions continued to torment Squirrel Sally. Yet no matter how hard she tried, she could not stop the vivid pictures from filling her mind.

Again she felt the desire to march across the wide street to the small café and start shooting at the men who had separated her beloved from his horse. Yet she knew that was not the way to help Iron Eyes.

'Gotta get that Doc Parry critter,' Sally silently whispered to herself through the pipe smoke that trailed from her lips. 'Ain't no point in finding that skinny bounty hunter full of holes without a quack in tow.'

'You say something, Missy?' Carter asked as he pushed the lead horse into position.

'Quit interfering,' Sally snapped as she pulled the pipe stem from her lips. 'I'm talking to myself. Ain't you ever talked to yourself?'

'Yep,' the blacksmith admitted. 'I'm usually the only critter that'll listen.'

In her short span of life, Sally Cooke had seen her entire family destroyed and taken from her. The feisty female was unable or unwilling to contemplate losing anyone else she loved.

'Hurry up, old timer,' she said, through clouds of tobacco smoke. 'I got me places to go and folks to kill.'

SEVEN

The clattering and distinctive sound of the stage-coach pulling up outside Doc Parry's log cabin alerted the medical man to the fact that he had a visitor. Parry dragged himself away from his breakfast and meandered from his kitchen, through his small office to the sturdy front door. He opened the door and stepped out on to the boardwalk and stared hard at the long vehicle in disbelief.

Parry scratched his unshaven chin and lowered his coffee cup from his lips and looked up at the handsome young female sat on the driver's board. He was about to smile at the petite female when he noticed the Winchester in her hands.

It was aimed straight at his unbuttoned vest.

'Get your bag and get in my stage, Doc,' Squirrel Sally ordered in a low ominous tone. 'We got us a long, hard journey to make.'

Parry raised the cup to his mouth and downed every last drop of the black beverage. He gave out a long sigh and then nodded at the very serious female.

He had no idea who she was or why she was sitting on the top of a stagecoach. All he recognized was the rifle in her hands and where it was aimed.

Doc Parry nodded. 'Be careful with that toothpick, young lady.'

Sally narrowed her eyes and frowned.

'I ain't no lady, Doc,' she snorted angrily, 'and this ain't no toothpick. I could shoot the buttons off your vest from here, but I won't. Not unless you decide not to come with me.'

The doctor cleared his throat. 'If I choose not to come with you? What'll you do?'

'I'll kill you,' Sally hissed. 'Savvy?'

Parry tossed the cup over his shoulder, leaned just inside his door and grabbed his battered old leather bag. He swiftly checked the inside of the bag and then snapped it shut and moved across the boardwalk and entered the coach. He had no sooner closed the door and sat down when he felt the vehicle jolt into action.

With his bag gripped in his hands, he felt the stage-coach gather speed as the sound of a bullwhip filled the air. Doc Parry gripped the wooden window tightly as he caught sight of the scenery moving faster and faster outside the accelerating body of the coach. Dust plumed up into the air off the vehicle's wheels as Sally screamed a series of obscene words at her team of horses.

Suddenly his dust-filled eyes spotted the trees to either side of the thundering stagecoach. He recognized the trail road only too well and knew of its solitary destination. Was she taking him to Fort Liberty? The thought chilled the man.

He had not been to the cavalry outpost since the Indian wars had started, and had no real desire to return there. He shook his head and vainly attempted to shake the cobwebs from his still sleepy brain. It normally took at least three cups of his powerful coffee before he would even dare to try and think this early in the morning, but he had only managed to consume one.

Doc Parry rocked back and forth on the padded bench seat as clouds of dust entered the confines of the coach and covered him and his medical bag. He rubbed it off his face as the stagecoach continued to travel between the trees along the wide logging road.

He knew that since the troubles had started, scores of small bands of Indians roamed the surrounding forests and fired their lethal arrows at anyone who had the misfortune of running into them. Parry had patched up a few of the unfortunate loggers, and signed the death certificates of twice as many others.

He gulped at the thought.

Most of the warriors were experts with their weaponry, and he had no wish to become their next target. Where was she taking him? The question kept nagging inside the medical man's quickly awakening mind. The veteran Parry watched helplessly as the trees whizzed past the windows of the coach. A thousand thoughts flashed through his mind. Who was this strange female? Parry could not recall ever seeing her in Bear Creek before. The blond female was not someone you forgot in a hurry. Why was she so determined that he come with her? So many questions and so few answers that made any sense.

The stagecoach bounced and sent him sliding on to the floor of the vehicle, still clutching his black bag. He heard his instruments clattering inside the leather casing as he scrambled back on to the padded seat. He wondered if he might require them before the day grew much older, but knew he would not discover anything about his abduction until the handsome rifle-toting girl decided to inform him.

Parry knew that he would find out soon enough.

Someone must be badly hurt, he reasoned. Why else would the fiery little female have kidnapped him? Unless she was one of those strange women he had read about in his medical books who just liked to collect random doctors. He swallowed hard at the thought. Squirrel Sally had seemed to be slightly less than rational, the more he thought about it.

In all his days, it was the first time he had been summoned at rifle point. Doc Parry felt a cold chill run down his backbone as he was thrown around the inside of the stagecoach like a rag doll.

Maybe she was crazy.

His knuckles grew increasingly white as he gripped the interior of the coach harder and harder. Parry wondered if he would be in any fit state to help anyone by the time she got him to wherever she was heading.

The six-horse team charged on.

EIGHT

A haunting mist hung a few feet above the trail road as the last of the night's frost finally evaporated. The crumpled body lay in a dried pool of blood exactly where it had landed after being propelled from the ornate Mexican saddle like a rag doll. The blood-soaked bounty hunter had not moved an inch as he battled with delirium and sank deeper into a place where reality and nightmares reigned.

Only his long bony fingers displayed any sign of life as they clawed like an eagle's talons at the sun-baked ground. It was as if some spark of life refused to obey a higher force and accept death.

Since losing his fight to stay conscious, the brutal rising sun had burned down on Iron Eyes' helpless form. Nothing could stop the bright rays from blistering his exposed flesh until it began to peel off his face and hands.

With every passing moment the sun grew hotter the further it rose into the blue cloudless sky. Eventually the pain of his burning skin began to stir the bounty hunter and draw him back from the jaws of death. Even in the depths of his own delirium, Iron

Eyes could feel the sun's rays burning the exposed portions of his flesh.

Iron Eyes slowly awoke, but still was unable to move a muscle. His bullet-coloured eyes returned from their hiding place under his scarred eyelids. For a while everything was blurred, but then slowly he began to focus across the trail road at the trees. To the famed hunter of wanted men they appeared like monsters towering over him.

But soon he realized what he was blankly staring at. Even in his dazed state, Iron Eyes knew that there was only one monster in this forest, and he was it. He had seen so many men and womenfolk recoil at the mere sight of his mutilated face over the years, and had grown to accept it.

Iron Eyes wore every fight and battle on his once normal features. They were evidence of his ongoing brutal battle with life itself. Most men would have died long before becoming the horrific sight he had turned into, but Iron Eyes was not like other men.

He had started to wonder whether the tall tales that various tribes of natives told of him were actually true. He should have died long ago, but somehow had managed to survive.

Perhaps it was true that even the Devil himself refused to accept the emaciated Iron Eyes into the fiery bowels of Hell, and kept sending him back into the realms of the living.

Iron Eyes attempted to move, but pain raced through his bruised and battered being and mocked his futile attempts. Soon it became evident to the gaunt bounty hunter that he was hurt badly. He craved whiskey, but in truth it was water he actually needed to help his dehydrated body as it lay helpless on the trail road.

His bullet-coloured eyes darted around the scene as his dazed mind raced in a bid to find some way of clawing himself back on to his feet. He wondered who had strung the saddle rope across his path and caused him to be ripped off the back of his trusty mount.

Then he wondered where the magnificent stallion was.

Had his prized horse been stolen? The question gnawed at his innards as he grew more and more angry.

Even though the bounty hunter was badly hurt he knew that he had to get off the ground. Yet every bone in his emaciated body ached like fury. It was as though he had just awoken from the torture chamber of his worst nightmares, but found his wrists still shackled by chains. Iron Eyes mustered every scrap of his will-power and forced his body to roll over on to his back.

Over the years Iron Eyes had been shot, knifed and clawed by various creatures of the wilderness. He bore the scars of every encounter on his thin body, but the pain that now tore through him as he lay on his back, matched them all.

For a moment he just lay there panting, like an old hunting hound. Every breath was agony to the pitifully lean bounty hunter, but Iron Eyes kept thinking of his precious palomino and how to get it back. That solitary thought fuelled his anger, and he knew that it was his only hope of survival. Vengeance would be his, he silently told himself. He would punish the men who had stolen his faithful horse, and make them pay the ultimate price.

Then he realized that he had moved his aching body into a far worse position by turning over. Now he was staring directly at the rising sun, with eyes that could no longer close due to the scarred skin that twisted the flesh of his face.

He sensed that his arms were not broken, but they were too weak to shield his unblinking eyes from the hypnotic rays of the merciless sun.

'Damn it all,' he cursed as he tossed his head from one side to the other in a vain bid to find refuge for his unprotected eyes.

Now the blinding sun continued to hit his mutilated face full on. There was nothing worse than facing a blazing sun with eyes that refused to close. His skull was filled with a mist that grew worse the longer his eyes stared at the blinding light.

There was no escape. The bright light seemed to get more and more intense with every beat of his pounding heart, as the stretched-out bounty hunter wriggled and squirmed beneath the relentless sun.

Iron Eyes carefully tried to straighten his long twisted body out of the crumpled heap it had become hours earlier when it had collided with the unforgiving ground. Yet every slight movement was agony.

The bounty hunter felt as though a hundred branding irons were being pressed into his body at exactly the same time from a hundred separate angles.

He gritted his teeth and pressed his hands on to the rough ground and summoned every scrap of his strength in order to force himself up off the rugged ground. He managed to raise his head and shoulders a few inches off the ground when a sudden pain tore through him like a cavalry sabre.

This pain was unlike anything his tormented body had ever experienced before. It was like being struck by a rod of venomous lightning.

Iron Eyes heard the pitiful squeal that emanated from his very soul and resounded off the surrounding trees. A hog being butchered would have sounded happier.

All thoughts of revenge vanished from his mind as the sharp, enduring pain persisted, until his matted mane of long black hair stretched out on the blood-stained ground. He was falling backwards again into the place that he had fought so hard to escape. Fog washed over his eyes in a sickening fashion as they continued to gaze upwards.

The swirling memory of Squirrel Sally briefly filled his dazed thoughts, but soon vanished into the abyss of blinding light, and sank without trace.

That was the last thing the brutalized bounty hunter remembered. Unconsciousness washed over him again. He attempted to fight the sickening mist that filled his throbbing head, but it was no use.

It was like leaping off a cliff into the rising vapour of a waterfall. He was totally helpless as he fell into that unknown place of tortured memories and thoughts. It was a place that he knew only too well, for he had visited it many times.

Like a corpse awaiting burial, Iron Eyes lay staring at the sun with unseeing eyes, unable to escape its wrath. A million notions flashed through his melting mind as he sank into a place where simple memories could become fiendish nightmares.

With each passing moment his fingernails clawed at the ground like talons, but he was helpless. He had never felt a pain like the one that tortured him, and he was defenceless against it.

Although he had lain on the ground ever since the horse thieves' saddle rope had propelled his lean body off the back of his palomino stallion, this time it was different. Until this moment he had slept without dreams tormenting him. Now his fevered mind was facing the sun, and he was unable to shield himself from its dangerous rays.

Now the peaceful sleep became a nightmare.

A tornado of confused memories mixed with the pain that racked his limp, motionless body. He continued to sink helplessly into the abyss of quicksand that his tortured mind created with every sharp breath.

Then suddenly there was peace.

Iron Eyes knew that death was clawing at his very soul in a vain attempt to finally take him into the bowels of Hell where there is no possibility of escape. Yet for some unknown reason the emaciated figure covered in dried blood no longer fought for his life.

The helpless bounty hunter was tranquil as he lay under the unrelenting sun as it blazed down upon his prostrate form. Iron Eyes had sunk into the depths of a million nightmares and long forgotten memories.

He no longer fought against the inevitable.

Every drop of his energy had been sapped from his stricken body as his mind wandered further and further away from his plight, back to a time when things had been very different.

As his mind drifted through the gathering fog, he saw something far ahead that he recognized. Slowly but surely the mist cleared until it was as sharp as anything he had ever seen before.

Iron Eyes stared at the image of himself when he was still young and handsome. A time when he had left the confines of his forested home and first ventured out into the place that is known as civilization.

It was a time when he was simply a young hunter who had survived by his wits and cunning alone against the forest Indians. A time before he was burdened by the scars with which countless battles had left him permanently branded.

Memories that were so vivid that they appeared more real than where the gaunt bounty hunter actually was. Stretched out on the hard ground.

The gaunt figure started to relive a less torrid time. A time when he had shared company with another female, not unlike the fiery Squirrel Sally. As the unconscious bounty hunter lay under the blistering rays of the sun, his memory became crystal clear and filled his helpless body with long-forgotten pictures and sounds.

Iron Eyes watched his past unfolding before him.

The unnamed forest where Iron Eyes had been abandoned as a baby and had grown to adulthood was no longer safe for anyone, apart from the various native tribes. It had become a treacherous place that the young Iron Eyes no longer felt safe to live in. After rescuing the beautiful raven-haired female called Ketna-Toi, or Fire Bird, she and the young man – known by the native Indians of the forest as Ayan-Es, the evil spirit – had barely escaped with their lives.

For his entire life, the youngster had taunted the Indians and moved through the trees unseen. He looted and robbed them of things he wanted, such as food and weapons. They had attempted to kill Iron Eyes many times, but the youth just mocked the Indians and thwarted them at every turn. This was the time when the tall stories of him became more and more vivid. They had begun to think of him as a ghost, whom it was impossible to capture or kill.

Iron Eyes could have remained in the forest had it not been for his valiant rescue of the beautiful Fire Bird. He knew that she would be instantly killed if she did not flee the massive forest. But the hunter could not allow the brutalized young Fire Bird to leave the forest and confront its dangers alone. Iron Eyes knew that beyond the trees it was probably even more dangerous.

They rode their stolen Indian ponies out from the dense forest into the unknown land that lay beyond its uncharted boundaries. Both were desperate to escape the wrath of the Indians – and yet the young hunter was spurred on by curiosity.

Iron Eyes had already ventured out into the world of the white men a few times, and realized it posed far more dangers than the forest for the innocent. These were dangers that his female companion would never comprehend, and which might be more perilous than anything she might expect in the forest.

A score of images flashed through the unconscious mind of the notorious bounty hunter. Yet he never caught even a glimpse of his own face. In those days the only time he ever saw himself was in the rippling reflection of a stream when he drank its precious liquid.

Yet he could see Fire Bird perfectly.

It was almost as if she were there. Not only could he see her, but he imagined that he could detect her scent. His memory shifted to how it had been as they had ridden from one town to another.

They had stood out like sore thumbs in the otherwise white world as they slowly headed due south. Both the Indian girl and Iron Eyes were unfamiliar with the habits and customs of this new culture.

Iron Eyes remembered how he had ventured into the logging town of Silver Creek several times and acquired a taste for both cigars and rot-gut whiskey, but his pretty companion had no knowledge of either poison.

The beautiful Fire Bird had been a virtual sacrificial slave to the Indians who roamed the forest, until she was saved by the young hunter from a fate far worse than he might have imagined. The bloody fight that had followed had claimed many victims, and when some of the liquored-up loggers from Silver Creek had tracked Iron Eyes into the forest, the tally grew even higher.

Red and white men locked horns and waged war within the confines of the forest. Blood ran freely from both sides – yet neither Iron Eyes nor Fire Bird ever discovered who had been victorious.

But that did not matter to either the hunter or the maiden.

All that mattered was that they kept heading away from the place where they had spent their entire lives. Iron Eyes kept seeing the vague image of himself as he lay prone on the blistering hot trail road.

The youthful Iron Eyes bore little resemblance to what he would eventually become. He was handsome, and yet still did not look like either the Indians or the white men he had already encountered.

His long black hair made him appear more like the Indians he had managed to outwit since he first began haunting their encampments. Yet it was obvious that the tall youngster was not of native blood. There was something different about Iron Eyes, which nobody had been able to fathom.

His streamlined features gave no hint as to his parentage.

The white men whom he had already encountered also bore little resemblance to the feral youngster. It seemed that Iron Eyes was somehow unique.

Basically he was unwelcome in either of their worlds.

Iron Eyes was a freak of nature who had been raised by wolves when the woodland creatures had discovered him as an abandoned baby. Somehow they had defied the odds and managed to nurture Iron Eyes into early youth. Then the Indians' arrows finally wiped out the only creatures who had ever cared for Iron Eyes. Their pelts hung on the teepee walls as trophies, and gave the young hunter even more reason to hate the Indians.

Until meeting up with Fire Bird, Iron Eyes had been totally alone. It had been far simpler then, he recalled. Iron Eyes found company a distraction, and not suited to his well-practised selfish nature.

The painfully lean Iron Eyes might have been travelling with a most attractive female, but he treated her with utter indifference. As the pair rode further and further south, the young female had wondered why her companion seemed unlike other men she had encountered. Most of the Indian men she had encountered had taken advantage of her, and she had grown to believe that they were all the same.

Yet days had turned to weeks since they had fled the forest, and Iron Eyes had not shown any interest in her, apart from curiosity.

Fire Bird wondered why.

In truth, Iron Eyes had only one thing on his mind, and that was food. He never stopped thinking about their next meal and how to catch, kill and cook it. Having had no experience of females in his entire life, he was blissfully unaware that they were different to menfolk in many ways.

He had not understood Fire Bird.

It was a trait that would haunt his entire life. Iron Eyes was troubled by womenfolk. To his straightforward mind, they were illogical.

The terrain had grown more familiar to the silent Iron Eyes as he steered his pony through the last of the tall grass toward the rolling hills, which seemed to go on forever. He drew on the crude rope reins and stopped his mount. Fire Bird moved her pony alongside him and halted.

She glared at him.

'Why are we stopping here, Iron Eyes?' she asked in her native tongue, a language that the young hunter had overheard many times over the years, and understood perfectly. 'This is not a good place to camp. Why do you stop here?'

Iron Eyes looked through the strands of his limp, long hair at the female who sat near him. She had pulled up the fringed hem of her rawhide dress to reveal her long, slim left leg, and she smiled unnervingly at the young hunter. He tilted his head and glanced at her thoughtfully. His eyes narrowed as he rubbed his stomach.

'I'm hungry,' he answered simply. 'I will kill food and you will cook it.'

The young Indian rolled her eyes and pulled her crude dress down over her thigh. She sighed heavily, and wondered how she could get his attention. His full attention.

'You want me to make camp?' she asked. 'A fire and a place for us to rest?'

Iron Eyes gave a nod. 'Make big fire. It is cold, and by the look of the stars it will get colder tonight.'

She could feel the cold breeze as it rolled over the hills and caused the tall grass to sway. Fire Bird looked ahead at the hills to where her companion was staring. Several trees covered each of the hills, yet she saw nothing edible. Fire Bird raised a perfect eyebrow.

'Where is the food?' she asked innocently. 'I see no food around here, Iron Eyes.'

Iron Eyes inhaled through his flared nostrils. 'Can you not smell it, Fire Bird?'

The beautiful female rolled her eyes.

'I smell land,' she sighed and teased. 'Grass, mud and trees. Are you thinking of eating them, Iron Eyes?'

'Make big fire,' Iron Eyes still had not understood her sense of humour, and frowned. He looped a leg over the neck of his mount and slid to the ground. He handed the rope rein to the smiling female and shook his head in confusion. 'Find kindling and stack it there.'

Fire Bird looked around. The sun was getting lower in the cloudless sky, and she estimated it would be dark in less than an hour.

'What do you smell, Iron Eyes?' she asked again as she dropped from her pony and secured the rope reins to a tree. She placed her knuckles on her hips and watched her companion long and hard.

'I smell game, Fire Bird,' he said, sniffing the evening air and looking back at her. He simply could not understand why she could not detect it. 'You have big nose. Why can it not smell game?'

'My nose is not big,' Fire Bird frowned and stared ahead at the scenery. Yet no matter how much she tried, she simply could not see any animal that her athletic companion might be able to trap.

'Are you sure?' she taunted her saviour.

Iron Eyes gave a firm nod. 'I am sure.'

Fire Bird shrugged and started plucking kindling off the ground and throwing it in a neat pile. 'Your nose is much bigger than mine. I think you can smell many things that I cannot.'

The lean youngster pulled the bow off his shoulder, then pulled an arrow from its quiver and placed it on the bow string; holding the silent weapon in one hand, he strode around the ponies and squinted at the closest outcrop of trees.

Iron Eyes looked over his shoulder at Fire Bird.

'Are you hungry?' he asked.

She gave a nod.

'Then get fire ready.' The tall young hunter walked like a mountain lion away from the two Indian ponies and Fire Bird towards the tree-topped hill. A lifetime of experience and endless practice ensured that his every step was silent. As he got nearer to the trees, Iron Eyes crouched down and his right arm pulled back on the bowstring until it was taut.

Suddenly he stopped, and then swung around on his boots until he was facing the opposite outcrop of trees. Without a moment's hesitation he fired.

The arrow flew straight and true and vanished from view in the tall, swaying grass close to the trees. There was a strange sound that briefly filled the air.

Fire Bird gasped in stunned surprise as she observed the speed and accuracy of her companion as he moved into the long grass towards the trees. Over the years the Indian maiden had seen many of her tribe hunting with bows, but none of them were as lethal as Iron Eyes.

It was uncanny.

The lean young hunter stopped and bent down. When he rose back up to his full height he was holding a prairie chicken in his hand. The stout bird was limp as Iron Eyes turned to face the feisty female. Iron Eyes waved the dead bird at his companion and then extracted the arrow from its rounded body and returned the deadly projectile to his quiver.

'Food.' He said triumphantly with a broad grin on his face as he shook the lifeless bird.

Fire Bird nodded in agreement. 'Food.'

NINE

The aroma of the freshly fried bird hung around the makeshift camp even though all that remained of the prairie chicken was a small pile of well sucked bones. Not a hint of the succulent fowl remained apart from its fragrance as the youthful Iron Eyes got up from the roaring flames and tossed the last of the gathered kindling into the heart of its flames. The fire perked up once more as flames climbed heavenward amid a thousand red embers and floated out across the desolate range. Iron Eyes cleaned his greasy hands with sand and then surveyed their surroundings.

The land seemed calm and peaceful, but the young hunter sensed something was wrong. Very wrong. A lifetime of experience warned Iron Eyes never to relax, and he always obeyed those feelings.

After fumbling through every pocket he finally located the last of his store-bought cigars buried deep in his shirt pocket. He straightened the black tobacco stick and placed it between his teeth. He lit the cigar with a length of kindling. Iron Eyes filled his lungs with the powerful smoke and then resumed his search of the surrounding terrain.

Iron Eyes said nothing as smoke filtered through his teeth.

'What is wrong, Iron Eyes?' Fire Bird had asked her tall travelling companion. Since fleeing the forest, she had grown to notice when the skilled hunter was anxious and not at ease.

The Indian maiden watched him as smoke trailed from his lips and vanished in the night air. He cast down his bullet-coloured eyes on her briefly before resuming their search. She patted the sand beside her.

'You are weary, my friend,' she said, with a tempting smile on her knowing face. 'Lie down and rest with me. You need sleep to cleanse your spirit.'

Iron Eyes did not reply.

He simply stood like a statue as his narrowed eyes scanned the surrounding terrain. The only movement from the young man, who would eventually become the most lethal bounty hunter, was his mane of long black hair as it flapped on his shoulders like the wings of an approaching bird of prey.

Fire Bird went to speak again but a glance down at her from the silent Iron Eyes stopped any questioning words from leaving his mouth. He stepped away from the campfire as sparks rose up into the black of the moonless sky. The female pulled her blanket over her small shoulders and carefully watched the man she secretly desired.

Since the pair had fled the forest the beautiful female had not seen Iron Eyes look the way he looked at this very moment, and that troubled her. There was genuine concern etched into his handsome features, but she had no idea what was troubling him. The young Indian could neither see nor hear anything.

Fire Bird went to ask him again what was wrong, but before she could speak, he pressed his long fingers against her lips and silenced her question.

Then Iron Eyes moved away from the campfire and drew his recently acquired six-shooters from his belt. As the guns hung at arm's length at his sides the young man continued to walk away from his companion. His eyes darted from one clump of trees to the next in search of his prey.

Every sinew in his tall body sensed that something was close and getting closer. Yet he had no idea who or what was headed towards the small camp. The dark sky hindered his keen eyesight, and only the flames from the fire behind his wide back illuminated the scattering of trees and swaying grass.

During his short existence he had encountered many wild animals and killed most of them. There was a rare type of deer in these parts. There were also various far more dangerous creatures as well. Mountain lions and bears were the most lethal animals in the forest, yet Iron Eyes did not sense their presence out here in the rolling hills.

Each creature that roamed the wilderness had its own scent, and yet his flared nostrils did not detect any of the countless animals he had hunted over the years.

Iron Eyes dropped down on to one knee and raised both his weapons. The skeletal youngster continued to listen as his ears heard movement nearby.

Something was out there, he silently thought.

But what?

The thought troubled Iron Eyes.

His eyes tightened as they vainly searched the strange sight before him. The flickering flames reflected off the tall grass and tree trunks like crimson phantoms and mocked his eyes. His fingers curled around the triggers of his guns as beads of sweat rolled down his brow and burned into his eyes.

Iron Eyes sniffed the night air like a hunting hound and realized that the scent was not that of a deer or other type of wild beast. His flared nostrils detected the unmistakable odour of white men.

Iron Eyes had learned quickly that they were probably the most dangerous animal of all because they killed without reason, unlike the beasts he was used to. White men enjoyed killing, unlike large wild cats or giant bears.

The young hunter heard dry kindling snapping under the weight of boot leather as his unseen foes advanced. His bony thumbs pulled back on his gun hammers until they locked into position.

His honed senses told him that there was more than one uninvited guest heading towards the temporarily campsite. At least two men were closing on Fire Bird and himself. Possibly more.

His long mane hung before his eyes. He stared through the limp strands of black hair as the evening breeze blew them back and forth before his unblinking eyes. As with most hunters, Iron Eyes had learned that to blink was to give the advantage to your adversary.

The lean hunter gritted his razor sharp teeth and glanced again back at Fire Bird sat beside the campfire. She was utterly unaware of the impending danger, which was getting nearer. He then returned his attention to the trees before him.

Whoever they were, they were closing in on the fiery beacon like moths to a flame. A scattering of notions flashed through his young mind. So far he had not detected the sound of horses apart from his own ponies. The uninvited intruders were on foot, and that gnawed at his craw.

Iron Eyes was well aware that horses were extremely valuable in the west, and many men of all hues would do anything to get their hands on them. He could see his pair of grazing Indian ponies out of the corner of his right eye. They were bathed in the dancing light of the fires flames.

Iron Eyes became even more concerned.

The lean young hunter knew that the animals were highly desirable to men on foot and most would do anything to obtain them. A cold shiver ran up his crouched backbone. His experience of white men was limited to those he had encountered in the town of Silver Creek, but that had been enough to alert Iron Eyes to the danger they posed.

As Iron Eyes pondered the impending encounter, Fire Bird suddenly let out a scream that filled the entire area. Startled, Iron Eyes swung around and saw his petite companion wrestling with two large men beside the campfire. Enraged, Iron Eyes went to rise to his full height when he heard another sound behind him. He turned and spotted two more heavily built men racing out from the trees toward him.

Before he knew it, they were upon him.

Iron Eyes went to fire his guns when a blinding flash of deafening fury sent him cartwheeling backwards. As his painfully lean body hit the ground the young hunter realized that he had been shot. The pain in his side hurt like nothing Iron Eyes had ever felt before.

As his head lay on the ground amid the tall grass, Iron Eyes could hear the men's boots as they advanced upon him. Hidden in the swaying wild grass, he raised both his guns and levelled them at the first of his attackers and squeezed the triggers of both his .45s.

Smoke billowed around the guns as red-hot flames carved through the darkness from the barrels. The first of the running men was halted as both shots hit him dead centre. He staggered and then tripped before crashing lifelessly beside the wounded Iron Eyes.

The other attacker paused in his tracks in disbelief at the sight of his companion's body stretched out close to the lean young hunter on the ground.

As Iron Eyes rolled on to his side he saw the standing man hauling his own gun from its holster and aiming down at him. In a fashion that he would one day perfect, the wounded young hunter cocked both six-shooters and fired again.

Two further shafts of ear-splitting venom spewed from the barrels of his smoking six-guns. At least one of Iron Eyes' bullets caught the second man high in his chest. The startled man dropped his gun and then toppled backwards like a felled tree.

Iron Eyes went to rise when tapers of scarlet fury cut through the surrounding air and passed within inches of him. He ducked and cocked his guns again and squinted at the other pair through the tall grass. He could see them clearly in the light of the campfire.

They still held the screaming Indian maiden.

Anger swelled up inside Iron Eyes. He could feel blood trailing down his side from the gash, and cocked both his guns again. He stared venomously through the high grass at the three people bathed in its eerie illumination.

As the pair of large men grappled with the terrified female between them, they continued firing their guns in the direction where they had last seen their chosen target fall.

With lethal lead passing only inches from him, Iron Eyes wanted to return fire, but he knew it would be impossible to pick off either of the men without hitting the screaming female. He was only too aware that he was still not experienced enough with fire-arms to trust his own accuracy.

He rolled through the tall grass until he was twenty feet away from the place where he had first dropped and then lay on his belly staring at them. Iron Eyes wanted nothing more than to kill the men who were taking advantage of the young maiden, just as he had killed the pair who had made the mistake of shooting him.

His eyes tightened.

The men were using the female to lure Iron Eyes out of his hiding place. He stared at the small group as Fire Bird bravely battled with her attackers until she was exhausted. Her small hands were no match for their relentless fists.

They were using her as a shield.

Iron Eyes released the hammers of his guns and rammed them into his crude belt. Defying the agony that tore through him, Iron Eyes started to crawl through the long swaying grass towards them.

As the wounded hunter drew closer to them, he peeled the bow off his shoulder and placed an arrow on its string. His eyes narrowed as they focused on the pair of ruthless men on either side of the breathless Fire Bird.

TEN

The raw graze on Iron Eyes' side was bleeding heavily as he stopped his advance and swallowed hard. Although the pair of attackers did not realize it, the injured young hunter had circled his raging campfire until he was barely thirty feet from where they were standing. Iron Eyes still had the ability to move on all fours when approaching his chosen prey. Just as the timber wolves had taught him before he realized he could walk upright as well.

Hunched in a striking position, Iron Eyes watched the two strangers as they wrestled with Fire Bird. The sharp pain along his ribs would not stop him, he vowed. It only honed his resolve as his fingertips touched the bullet wound, and his eyes narrowed and glared through the shimmering flames.

Only the campfire stood between the loathsome opportunists and the watchful Iron Eyes. The fire had somehow drawn the dregs of humanity to its bright flames in search of the pair of Indian horses bathed in the flickering light.

The wounded young hunter could not give a damn why the quartet found themselves on foot. All his inexperienced mind could think about was the fact that they had done so and attempted to kill him. For that outrage, he would make them pay the ultimate price.

Iron Eyes eased his lean torso on to the sandy ground and peered through the tall ocean of swaying grass. His bony hand turned the small bow so its arrow had a clear shot through the grass before him.

Iron Eyes gripped the body of the bow as his left index finger curled around the shaft of the arrow sat upon its taut string. His right hand had already drawn the string back as he held the arrow's feathered flight between his thumb and fingers, as he watched the two large figures manhandling the angry young maiden between them. An unfamiliar feeling started to smoulder deep inside him, which Iron Eyes did not recognize or understand.

It was a feeling he had no knowledge of.

All he knew for sure was that it was growing more intense the longer he watched the unknown duo hurting the beautiful young Indian girl.

He wanted to kill them.

This was an emotion that was alien to him. He had always killed when he was hungry. The wolves had taught him that skill, but he had never felt the desire to kill when he was not hungry.

Her pitiful screams seemed to make him even angrier with the horse thieves. Iron Eyes had little experience with humanity, and was still learning how to cope with these strange feelings that tormented him. He had only ever observed how people reacted to one another from a distance. Now since rescuing Fire Bird a tidal wave of emotions was battering his naïve feral mind.

He held the arrow in readiness as his focus remained on the last of their attackers. The campfire was still bright enough to cast its faltering light on the three individuals standing behind its curtain of flames.

With droplets of sweat trailing down his face, Iron Eyes glared through the flames at the two men and the captive Indian maiden held between them.

Iron Eyes still could not understand why this was making him so angry. Why was this any different to watching an eagle taking a wild dove out of the sky, bringing it to the ground and tearing it to bits?

It made no sense to the young hunter.

The flames mocked his keen eyes as he attempted to get a clear target through the campfire. The unsteady image of the very different trio made it virtually impossible for Iron Eyes to see his targets with any clarity.

He summoned every drop of his dwindling strength and watched the three people as they shuffled back and forth. The last thing he wanted to do was end up hitting Fire Bird and not one of her captors.

The young hunter had known that they would not release their grip on Fire Bird willingly for she was their shield and would prevent her companion from shooting. Yet the longer Iron Eyes waited, the less chance she had of surviving.

As a hunter, Iron Eyes had never hesitated before. Normally he would fire his weapon as soon as he caught sight of his target. He could not explain why he was so unwilling to unleash the arrow.

Why was he so troubled at the thought of hitting her?

He simply did not understand.

Iron Eyes rested his head on his outstretched arm; he gasped heavily for a few moments until he had composed himself. Every part of his body hurt as he slowly raised his head and stared again through the shimmering flames.

He watched as they raised their six-guns and started firing at the spot where they had last seen him when he was knocked off his feet by the shot that had glanced off his ribs.

Both men blasted their bullets into the tall grass and then paused to reload their guns. They were obviously confused that there was no reply to their relentless shots, and hadn't been for over five minutes. Iron Eyes got to his knees and stared at the bewildered pair across the campfire. He could tell that they had started to wonder why their tall target had fallen silent.

'You reckon we hit that skinny varmint, Luther?' one of them asked his companion. 'He quit blasting his guns a while back now. Maybe he's dead.'

His partner was less sure.

'I ain't so sure,' the other said as he expertly reloaded his six-shooter. 'He might just be playing possum.'

'We already seen Fred and Saul shoot him down,' the snorting man said as he held Fire Bird firmly. 'We both unloaded our guns into the grass where he fell. He gotta be dead.'

'I still ain't convinced.'

As the horse thieves continued to talk, Iron Eyes forced himself up off the ground and crouched, nursing the bow and arrow in his hands. He summoned up every scrap of his flagging strength and stood.

Only the flames and smoke separated them.

For a few moments neither of the men noticed the haunting vision through the flames as they snapped their six-guns back into readiness and were about to resume firing at their distant target. Then as the shortest of the pair tightened his hold on Fire Bird unceremoniously around her chest and swung her around, Iron Eyes released his arrow.

The lethal projectile went straight through the flames and smoke and homed in on its target. It found it in less than a heartbeat.

A hideous scream bellowed out from the horse thief as he reeled in agony and released his hold on Fire Bird. The feisty female wriggled and fought like a wild cat with the last of her attackers as he stared in disbelief at his dying companion.

'Help me, Luther,' he croaked.

As one man fell, the other swung around on his boot leather and caught sight of the wounded Iron Eyes through the wall of flames as the young hunter stood defiantly watching the final horse thief.

Iron Eyes dropped his bow and glared at his opponent. The night breeze blew his mane of long black hair off his face as his bullet-coloured eyes maintained their focus on the burly figure.

With the arrow buried deep in his chest, the shorter of the rustlers dropped to the ground. The last horse thief watched in stunned horror as his partner rolled lifelessly on to his back with blood pumping from the savage wound.

Then Fire Bird managed to pull free of his grip and threw herself at the ground a few yards away from where he stood.

Luther Jacobs and his small gang of rustlers had spent more than two years in this part of the country killing and stealing before they had spotted Iron Eyes and his companion earlier that day. The gang had left their own mounts back at their camp over the rolling hills before setting out to relieve the young riders of the ponies. It was a task they had done many times before without incident.

Jacobs could not fathom how this well practised action had gone so terribly wrong as he returned his icy stare to the tall figure of Iron Eyes.

Filled with shocked outrage, Jacobs stared through the flames at the young hunter and raised his .45. He aimed at the windswept figure and eased his gun hammer back until it clicked loudly.

The night air filled with the sound of the cocked six-shooter.

'I don't know who you are, fella,' Jacobs shouted at the tall lean youngster as his shaking hand tried to aim. 'But you're gonna pay for killing my boys. Pay with your damn life, you worthless bastard.'

The words did not deter the resolve that Iron Eyes felt surging through his veins as he tightened his stare on the bellowing Jacobs. His long slim fingers drifted back to the leather scabbard hanging on his hip. He pulled his long knife from it and gripped the bone grip tightly.

Suddenly a deafening blast from Jacobs' gun barrel sent a lethal bullet through the smoke. It carved a hole in the smoke as it sought the young Iron Eyes.

As he had done numerous times before when avoiding the deadly arrows of the forest Indians, Iron Eyes simply leaned slightly sideways so the bullet passed his head. He felt the heat of the deadly chunk of lead as it passed within inches of his face. Without uttering a word to the horse thief, the tall hunter threw the long-bladed knife with all his might. The blood-stained blade headed through the smoke and flames at Jacobs before his thumb had time to haul back on his gun hammer again.

The knife hit Jacobs dead centre.

A guttural groan escaped the gang leader's mouth as his eyes looked down in horror at the knife buried up to its hilt in his chest. Jacobs staggered backwards a couple of steps as he watched blood suddenly surround the knife and spread across his shirt front.

Luther Jacobs went to speak, but only blood left his lips.

His eyes returned to the pitifully lean young hunter as he felt the six-shooter fall from his hand. He stared in horror as Iron Eyes drew one of his guns from his belt, cocked it and began to raise his hand until it was level with the horse thief. Luther fell on to his knees and watched helplessly as Iron Eyes aimed at his head.

'Now it is your turn to die,' Iron Eyes whispered.

But before Iron Eyes had time to squeeze the six-gun's trigger, the stricken Jacobs fell forwards on to his face.

Iron Eyes released his gun hammer and returned the .45 to his belt. The wounded young hunter gritted his teeth and walked around the rising flames until he was stood above both of the bodies.

Without emotion, he pulled the arrow from one of the bodies and pushed it into the quiver on his hip. Iron Eyes then leaned over Jacobs. His bony hands flipped the body on to its back and extracted his bloody knife from Jacobs' chest.

Fire Bird silently watched as her strange travelling companion wiped the gore off the knife blade and then slid it into its scabbard.

Iron Eyes remained silent as he stepped over the bodies and walked to the side of the female. He took her hand, pulled her off the sand and then sat down where she had been watching the unfolding events.

It was only then that she noticed that the side of his clothing was drenched in blood. His own blood.

'You are hurt.' She exclaimed and dropped down next to him and stared at the blood, which was visibly trailing from the deep graze that stretched across his ribs. 'You are hurt bad.'

Iron Eyes nodded silently in agreement.

ELEVEN

Iron Eyes could feel a steady stream of blood trickling from the savage bullet wound on his side. It hurt like hell. He lay back and rested his head on the sand as Fire Bird feverishly tended his wound. As she worked to stop the bleeding, his bullet-coloured eyes stared at the pair of bodies near the campfire. Even after fighting for his life with their attackers, Iron Eyes could still not understand what motivated these men. During his lifetime he would not become any wiser when it came to the white men who roamed this once pristine land.

The gaunt young hunter pushed the concerned Indian maiden away, but Fire Bird was not so easy to dissuade. She grabbed his hands and frowned into his face.

'Stop, Iron Eyes,' she snorted in her native tongue firmly.

The fearsome hunter stared through his limp black hair at her and shrugged. He sighed.

'I do not understand the white eyes,' he reluctantly admitted to his companion as he attempted to rise. 'They want things that do not belong to them.'

She placed the palm of her hand on his exposed chest and pushed him backwards. Fire Bird was far stronger than she looked, he thought. He was surprised.

'What do you want?' he groaned.

'I will help you, Iron Eyes,' she said as she carefully pulled his shirt away from the bleeding graze that had torn his flesh from his ribs. 'I have tended the wounds of many warriors. I know how to stop the bleeding. It will hurt, though.'

He glanced down at the blood. 'It already hurts.'

Her impish expression twinkled in the fire light.

'That is good, Iron Eyes,' she grinned. 'If it didn't hurt, you would be dead.'

Iron Eyes recalled smiling as his beautiful companion fed the fire with more kindling and placed the blade of his own knife in its flames.

'Why are you burning my knife?' he had asked her.

Fire Bird knew that wounds like the one that her fearless companion had suffered could be treated in many ways, but first the bleeding needed to be stemmed. The handsome female pushed the blade deeper into the hot embers until its steel began to glow.

'I must melt your skin,' she had told him bluntly.

'Melt?' he had repeated as he tried to understand what she meant. Soon he would learn exactly what she was trying to say.

For more than ten minutes the female cleaned the wound of all the grit and debris it had picked up during his crawling through the rough terrain.

Then without hesitating for even a heartbeat, Fire Bird withdrew the knife from the flames, turned and pressed its hot metal blade against his bleeding flesh.

The young hunter shook in stunned horror.

The smell of roasting flesh filled his flared nostrils as unimaginable pain tore through his scrawny body. Iron Eyes yelled out in agony. He then recalled succumbing to unconsciousness as the white-hot knife did its job and melted his flesh until the bleeding finally stopped.

As the brutal memories of an earlier time faded back into the fog of his injured mind he heard another voice in the distance. A voice that was utterly different to that of Fire Bird, but just as familiar. The voice grew louder and louder as it penetrated the protective walls of his befuddled brain and reached into his very soul.

It was the voice of Squirrel Sally.

Then Iron Eyes felt his head being knocked from one side to the next as a hand slapped his cheeks violently. His eyes rolled down from their hiding place in his skull and stared straight at the fiery female straddling his chest.

'Iron Eyes,' she repeated over and over again as she continued slapping his face. 'Wake the hell up.'

The bounty hunter coughed and gritted his teeth as his icy stare glared angrily at the golden-haired female straddling his chest.

'Get off me, Squirrel,' he rasped.

Sally looked down at her beloved Iron Eyes and beamed. She then quickly got off him and clambered to her feet. Without pausing for breath, the female ran to the carriage of her stagecoach.

She almost ripped the door off its hinges as she opened it and glared at the terrified Doc Parry huddled on one of the vehicle's padded bench seats.

'Get out here, Doc,' Sally ordered.

Parry was about to comply when he felt her grab his arm in a firm grip and haul him out into the sunlight. As his feet hit the ground, the female pushed him towards Iron Eyes' stretched out body.

'Oh, my dear Lord,' the doctor exclaimed as he stared down at the pitiful bounty hunter. 'Who killed this poor wretch?'

'He ain't dead,' Sally shouted. 'He always looks like that.'

'He does?' Doc Parry gulped.

Squirrel Sally retrieved his black bag, thrust it into his hands, and then pushed him closer. She pointed at Iron Eyes and pushed her ample body close to Parry.

'Fix my betrothed,' she hissed into his stiff collar. 'Get doctoring.'

Parry gave a nod of his head and fearfully obeyed the snarling female. He dropped on to his knees and opened his bag and withdrew his stethoscope. He swiftly placed the ivory end of the tube on Iron Eyes' chest and listened.

'My goodness,' the doctor remarked. 'He is alive.'

'Sure I'm alive,' Iron Eyes hissed like a rattler.

Sally clambered up the side of her stagecoach to the driver's high seat, reached down into its belly and produced a bottle of whiskey from its depths. She turned and leapt like a puma.

The alarmed medical man heard her bare feet land solidly back on to ground a few feet from where he silently worked on his patient.

'How is he, Doc?' Sally asked before extracting the cork from the bottle's neck.

'I'm OK,' Iron Eyes said.

'Hush up,' Squirrel snapped at the bounty hunter before turning to Parry and repeating her question. 'How is he, Doc?'

'He ain't dead, Missy,' Parry's knowing hands inspected the body speedily before his eyes noticed Sally's shadow bearing down on both himself as well as Iron Eyes. Parry turned his head and watched as the tiny female took a swig of the amber liquor and then burped. 'No broken bones.'

Sally frowned. 'What you say?'

'I said, he's not broken anything,' Parry announced. 'He's just been knocked senseless. The cut on the back of his skull has already dried up, like the wound on his belly.'

Sally leaned over and peered into the doctor's eyes.

'Is you telling me this long stretch of bacon is okay?' she asked, as his expression changed when he noticed her sweating cleavage before his face. Parry did not reply as a satisfied smile started to cross his face.

Sally looked down at the medical man staring open-mouthed at her swaying breasts barely concealed by her ripped and tattered shirt. She slapped him just hard enough for his eyes to look up into her frowning features.

'Was you looking at my chests?' she asked.

He nodded. 'I am a doctor. I can say that you are very healthy, young lady.'

'I asked you a question, Doc,' she growled and stomped her foot. 'I asked you if my man there is okay. Is he?'

Doc nodded. 'He'll be fine. He's badly shaken and injured, but he'll pull through.'

Sally straightened up and looked around the scene. It then occurred to the youthful female that her beloved Iron Eyes must have been knocked off the back of his trusty palomino. That had to be it, she thought. That was how the two horse thieves got their hands on the golden stallion.

'That makes sense, Doc,' she mumbled before stepping over the bounty hunter. She crouched down quickly and tore the knees out of her pants in the process. She stared down at the man she was inexplicably drawn to, and placed the whiskey bottle next to his head. The aroma of the strong liquor made his nostrils flare as they sniffed the air. 'He's lucky them horse thieves didn't shoot him.'

Doc Parry slowly got back to his feet and dusted himself off. He then picked up his medical bag and closed its wide open jaws to protect its contents. He was still as confused as he been when the feisty female had arrived at his cabin hours earlier.

'What horse thieves?' he blurted out in honest ignorance.

112

Squirrel Sally did not answer his question, for she had other things on her mind. The relief that Iron Eyes was still alive was almost more than she could cope with.

Parry watched her mane of long golden curls suddenly cover the bruised and battered head of the bounty hunter as she pressed her lips on to the scarred mouth of Iron Eyes. The embarrassed medical man cleared his throat and diverted his eyes to his side and the stagecoach. When he heard the unmistakable sound of lips parting he returned his attention to the petite young woman.

He watched as Iron Eyes slowly raised a hand. Sally thought he wanted to hold her hand and attempted to grab it. But Iron Eyes did not want to hold her hand – he wanted to get hold of the whiskey bottle beside his head.

'Do you feel better, darling?' she sighed heavily.

'Whiskey,' the bounty hunter managed to say. 'Gimme that damn bottle of whiskey, Squirrel.'

'Is you thirsty, beloved?'

Iron Eyes rubbed his mouth with skeletal fingers. 'Nope. I just got this weird taste in my mouth. Don't know what it is, but it sure is awful.'

Snorting, Sally pushed the open bottle into his hand and then got back to her feet. She stared down at him as he started to drain the bottle of its fiery contents, and then shook her head.

'I kissed you, Iron Eyes,' she stated with a stomp of her right foot. 'That's the taste of a mighty ripe woman you're trying to wash down your damn gullet.'

Iron Eyes tossed the empty bottle aside and then looked at both her and the demure doctor. He raised a busted eyebrow, and then began to get to his feet.

Parry helped his strange patient rise to his full height and bit his lip silently. He had the wisdom to remain quiet as the tall bounty hunter rested against the side of the stagecoach and ran his bony fingers through his matted hair.

'Somebody stole my horse,' Iron Eyes groaned as he slowly checked his pockets. 'I think there was two of them. They must have figured I was dead when I hit the ground.'

'Take it easy, young man,' Parry advised the tall bounty hunter. 'You'll need plenty of rest, but you'll be fine in a few days.'

Iron Eyes' icy stare darted to the small medical man.

'I ain't got a couple of days, Doc,' he snorted. 'I got to find them bastards and get my horse back.'

Doc Parry decided wisely not to argue.

'I already got your horse back, you cracker barrel,' Sally said as she strode to the side of the bounty hunter. With knuckles on her hips Sally stared up at him, and sighed again.

Iron Eyes glanced down at her.

'You what?' he queried.

'That damn palomino is tied to the back of my stagecoach, Iron Eyes,' Sally informed the shaken bounty hunter as he continued to pat his pockets in search of a cigar. 'Take a look if you don't believe me.'

114

Iron Eyes took two long steps and stared at his golden stallion secured to the stagecoach boot. He rubbed his eyes, in case they were lying to him. Then he turned to Sally and gave a thankful nod.

'I'm obliged, Squirrel,' he said, as her small hand gifted him with a black twisted cigar. Iron Eyes placed the cigar between his teeth and pulled a match from a pocket.

As his thumbnail scratched the tip of a match and ignited the cigar with its flame the haunting bounty hunter began to feel better. He turned his neck until it clicked, and then blew the flame out with a line of grey smoke. He patted the neck of his prized stallion and watched as Parry quietly got back into the body of the coach.

Sally moved closer to her tall associate and watched him savour the smoke he inhaled. She toyed with his tattered shirt front and fluttered her eyelashes at him, yet Iron Eyes did not appear to notice.

Frustrated, the tiny female pressed herself into him until his icy stare looked down at her. He extracted the cigar from his lips and tilted his head.

'What you want, Squirrel?' he asked, through clouds of smoke.

'Didn't you like my kiss?' Sally questioned in a tone which was threatening. 'It woke you up. You was mumbling and jabbering all sorts of rubbish until our lips met.'

'I thought it was you hitting my face that jerked me awake,' he argued.

Sally fluttered her eyelashes. 'Nope, it was my kissing.'

Iron Eyes raised an eyebrow.

'What was I saying, Squirrel?' he wondered, as he recalled the memories that had reawakened while he was unconscious. 'Anything good?'

Her expression suddenly changed. She had the look of surprised shock on her dusty face as she started to think about it more clearly.

'Before you yelped like a hog in a slaughter house, you did say a few words, but I'm damned if I know what they meant, sweetheart,' Sally purred as she continued to press her breasts into him. 'I reckon they was just nightmares and suchlike.'

Iron Eyes drew smoke into his lungs again as he tried to peel her away from him. 'Yeah, I guess I was just having a bad dream.'

Squirrel Sally frowned. 'That must be it. You was muttering about birds and fire and all sorts of loco things.'

'Fire Bird,' Iron Eyes repeated the words and remembered the name of another beautiful young female who had been very similar to Sally. He smiled and began to nod. 'You're right. They're just the ravings of a mighty confused mind, Squirrel.'

Sally hugged the tall bounty hunter. 'Doc said you need a rest, Iron Eyes. I'll take you back to town and you can have yourself some grub and we can rent a room.'

Horrified at the thought of being cornered in a rented room with the overly excited female, the scrawny bounty hunter pushed her away from him and began to check his high-withered stallion for any injuries. He paused at the saddlebags and located his precious stash of whiskey bottles.

Sally watched as he withdrew one of the full vessels and extracted its cork with his teeth and spat it away. After a long swallow of the powerful liquor, he paused and looked hard at her.

'Where in tarnation did you find this horse, Squirrel?' he wondered before adding: 'And how did you get it away from them varmints?'

Squirrel pouted. 'I took it from where they left it.'

Iron Eyes felt the cigar being pulled from his lips, and watched as she placed it in her own mouth and started puffing like a locomotive.

'You stole it from the varmints that stole it from me?' he asked, before raising the bottle and downing a third of its contents in one long swallow. 'Is that it?'

'Damn right,' Sally winked and giggled. 'They're sure gonna be angry when they find out what I done.'

Iron Eyes was thoughtful as he lowered the whiskey bottle from his mouth, and rubbed his scarred lips with his thumb. He handed the bottle to his companion and pulled the stallion's reins free of the stagecoach tailgate.

'What you doing, Iron Eyes darling?' she asked, as she realized that the gaunt bounty hunter was about to mount his powerful stallion. 'Get in the coach and rest. I'll take you into town with the Doc.'

Iron Eyes halted with the long reins in his bony grip and stared down at his affectionate friend. It was hard for anyone to fathom what the painfully lean bounty hunter was thinking due to his maimed features, but the small Sally was better at it than most. She was capable of seeing through his many scars and reading him like an open book.

'Them horse thieves ain't the sort of varmints to shrug off being bested by a girl, Squirrel,' Iron Eyes mumbled before plucking the cigar from her lips and ramming it back into his own mouth. 'They'll want this horse back so they can sell it. They'll be gunning for both of us once they get wise to what's happened. I gotta stop them before they kill us.'

Sally watched as her beloved friend raised a leg, rammed a boot into the stirrup and mounted the muscular stallion. The gaunt bounty hunter looked far too weak to go looking for a fight, but he seemed determined to do so.

'You ain't in no fit condition to go fighting them critters, Iron Eyes,' she blurted as desperation welled up in her heart. 'You can't go fighting right now.'

Silently, Iron Eyes gathered up his reins in his bony hands and turned the palomino stallion. He knew she was right, but every bone in his aching body told him that he had to face the pair and destroy them.

He glanced over his broad shoulder at her.

'Where are they?' he asked.

'The blacksmith told me they went to a café,' Sally informed the gaunt horseman. 'He said he heard them saying that they were going to rest up in the hotel after they'd eaten.'

'They gotta be at the hotel then,' Iron Eyes reasoned.

'Reckon so,' Sally nodded. Her long golden curls enveloped her face so that he could not see the tears that were welling up in her blue eyes before running down her dusty cheeks.

Iron Eyes slowly nodded at her. Then he drove his spurs into the flesh of his mighty horse and thundered away towards Bear Creek. Dust rose up into the sunlight as it kicked off the horse's hoofs.

The stallion had barely travelled a hundred yards when Sally spun on her heels, ran down the length of the stagecoach and with the whiskey bottle gripped in one hand, climbed up on to her driver's seat. She picked up her corncob pipe and clenched its stem with her perfect teeth as she unlooped the long leather reins off the brake pole.

'You ain't getting away from me that easy,' Sally said as a steely determination etched her handsome features. She rubbed the tears from her eyes and nodded firmly. 'I'm gonna stop that long streak of bacon from getting himself killed, even if it means killing them galoots myself.'

With the open bottle clenched between her thighs splashing its fiery contents in all directions, Sally clenched her pipe stem in her teeth and got her six-horse team moving in unison until they were able to pursue her beloved Iron Eyes.

'I'm gonna help that dumb scarecrow even if he don't want any help,' she growled as the body of the coach rocked on its springs in the blistering sunlight. 'He ain't fit enough to go fighting them horse rustlers on his lonesome.'

Sally cracked her bullwhip over the heads of her six horses and then grappled with the heavy leather reins as she physically controlled the muscular team below her high perch.

As choking trail dust kicked up from the horses' hoofs and the rotating wheels, Doc Parry poked his head out of the carriage window, looked up and croaked as loudly as he dared to the beautiful driver of the weathered stagecoach.

'What's happening, Missy?' he called out from the interior of the rocking vehicle as Sally expertly handled the long vehicle. In less than a minute she had turned her six-horse team full circle until it was aimed in the direction of the logging town. 'Who are you talking to?'

The pounding hoofs of the team resounded around the trees which flanked the stagecoach as it thundered along after the badly injured bounty hunter. All four wheels left the rough ground as it hurtled across the crudely fashioned road. Sally heard the distressed doctor bouncing around inside the body of the vehicle, and laughed out loud.

'I'm talking to myself, Doc,' Squirrel Sally lashed the hefty reins down on the backs of her team and shouted at the top of her voice as the stagecoach began to gather pace. 'There ain't nobody else worth wasting talk to up here.'

The medical man clung on for dear life as the contents of the stacked boxes spilled over him. He shook his head and muttered.

'I knew I should have had me another cup of coffee,' he moaned. 'This is getting painful.'

Sally curled her toes around the wooden frame of the driver's box and cracked the bullwhip again. She could still see the hoof dust ahead of her charging horses and could make out the pitifully weak bounty hunter clinging to the powerful palomino stallion. A wry grin covered her dust-caked face when she realized that she was gaining on her beloved. Sally leaned sideways from the high seat, looked down at the side of the coach, and then yelled to her helpless passenger.

'You'd best hang on to something, Doc,' she shouted to the doctor as she heard him collide with the coach floor. 'Hang on for your life.'

TWELVE

The late afternoon sun was starting to fade as it slowly headed down into the forest to end another day. It was still bright, though, as the sky reflected its dying embers across the heavens above Bear Creek. Both Snider and Mason had rested in the hotel room for hours until instinct dragged one of them from his slumbers: the younger of the outlaws rolled off his bed and alerted his partner that something was wrong. Jeb Snider was visibly shaken by the vivid nightmare that had tormented his rest since he had fallen asleep. But Bren Mason was angry that he had been awoken by nothing more than a bad dream.

The outlaws made their way down into the hotel lobby, but the older of the horse thieves was growing angrier with every step as they headed down toward the hotel lobby.

'Why'd you wake me up, Jeb?' Bren Mason snarled as he followed his partner out into the blazing rays of the setting sun. 'I was having me a real nice dream. How come you woke me up, you pinhead?'

The heat of the day was still rising from the sand that it had roasted since sun-up, and it caused both outlaws to pause beneath the welcome shade of the porch overhang. The temperature did not calm the situation between the men. Mason was still eyeing his partner angrily.

'I asked you a damn question, Jeb,' Mason growled as he stared at his shaking companion. 'You look like you seen a ghost or something.'

'Quit moaning, Bren,' Snider snapped back. 'I had me the weirdest dream. Something's wrong, I tell you.'

Mason gave out a guttural laugh. 'Don't tell me you suddenly became a witch. Where's your crystal ball, partner?'

The brooding pair stood, one at each end of the hotel boardwalk, and rested their thumbs on their holsters. The younger Snider was bathed in beads of sweat – a sweat that had encouraged the horse thief to rise, as it added to a strange premonition that had haunted his dreams and turned them into a nightmare.

Snider rested his hand on the wooden upright as his grumbling companion meandered to his side. He glanced at Mason as the veteran outlaw scratched a match into flame and ignited the cigar hanging from his lips.

'You ever had a feeling clawing at your insides, Bren?' Snider asked as he watched the match flicked from his partner's fingers as smoke drifted from his mouth. 'I mean a real bad feeling that just won't quit?'

Mason narrowed his eyes and stared at Snider.

'You woke me up 'coz you had a bad dream?' he snarled through the smoke, and shook his fist. 'I ought to beat the juice out of you, Jeb boy.'

Snider turned to face his partner in crime.

'I reckon we should check the livery,' he said bluntly. 'I got the strangest feeling that something's wrong.'

Mason shook his head in despair and then shrugged.

'You're plumb loco, Jeb,' he riled before stepping down off the boardwalk and heading towards the massive structure set at the end of the wide street. 'But I'll humour you. C'mon, let's go see if that palomino is okay.'

Snider followed his partner towards the livery stable. He could not understand it himself, but he found it impossible to shake off the feeling of impending doom that was gripping his guts like a poison.

'I can't figure it, Bren,' Snider announced as he trailed the older of the outlaws towards the livery stable. 'I ain't never felt like this before. Something is wrong, though. I just know it.'

Mason glanced over his shoulder at his partner.

'If there ain't nothing wrong, Jeb,' he started, and then warned his companion, 'I'm gonna pound you into dust. You're gonna pay for waking me up like that.'

Both men were still arguing when they entered the vast livery stable a few moments later. The interior of the structure was far darker than the street. It took a few moments for their eyes to adjust and enable them to see clearly.

But it was what they couldn't see which troubled them the greatest.

Mason stood gripping the cigar between his teeth as his eyes searched every stall for the distinctive palomino stallion. He saw their own saddle mounts in stalls close to the large barn doors, but there was no sign of the valuable golden horse.

Snider turned on his boot leather as he, too, looked for the powerful horse. Finally he stopped turning and looked straight at Mason.

'Where's the horse?' he asked his partner breathlessly.

Mason pulled the cigar from his lips and angrily tossed it at the sand at their feet.

'That's what I was thinking, Jeb,' he growled through the last of the smoke that peppered his every word. 'Where's that horse?'

'This is just like my dream,' Snider countered in astonishment.

Mason crushed the cigar under his boot leather and then took a step into the livery. Yet no matter how far he ventured, there was no sign of the valuable palomino stallion.

'Hush up about your damn dream, Jeb,' he snarled.

Snider took a few steps closer to the blacksmith's forge and looked all around the barn's vast interior. There were several horses in stalls, but not the distinctive one they were seeking. He raised an arm and pointed to a corner.

'Weren't there a stagecoach by that loft ladder?' he muttered before glancing back at Mason. 'I'm sure I saw a stagecoach over there when we handed our horses to that liveryman this morning.'

Mason moved to his partner. 'Where is the black-smith? How come he ain't here?'

Frantically, Snider rubbed his neck as he again searched the massive structure fruitlessly. He then exhaled loudly and bit his lower lip as his eyes returned to the fuming Mason.

'What you thinking, Bren?' he asked.

'Hell, I don't know what to think, Jeb,' Mason growled like a bear with a sore head and headed towards the forge. A few glowing coals still remained in the brick pit. 'Our valuable stallion ain't nowhere to be found, and neither is the blacksmith. To my way of thinking, this is mighty suspicious.'

Snider rubbed his face with his gloved hands.

'Maybe that old liveryman figured he'd do exactly what we was going to do and sell that palomino him-self, Bren,' he reasoned.

Mason's eyes tightened as the notion sank into his festering brain like molten magma. He reached up and gripped the forge pump before dragging it down towards him. The coals suddenly began to glow more intensely in the brick forge beside him. He repeated the action until scarlet sparks rose up and floated into the metal chimney stack fixed directly above the circular forge.

'You might be right, Jeb boy,' he hissed as he con-tinued to pump the lever until every grey coal brick transformed into a mass of glowing crimson. 'But that blacksmith didn't look the sort of varmint to get greedy.'

As they mulled over the problem they both heard a sudden noise behind their backs. They swiftly turned and looked into the darkest corner of the livery stable as a door beside the last stall opened and the brawny blacksmith entered.

Joe Carter was a simple, honest character but he sensed the danger that he was about to face. But even though he was scared he did not miss a step, and continued towards the wanted men as they stood beside his forge.

He remained silent as he slowly approached them, and only stopped when he reached the gap between Mason and Snider. His rippling muscles glinted in sweat as he looked at both men in turn. The liveryman wondered what their reaction would be when they discovered what had actually happened to their precious palomino. He dried the sweat off his brow with his hairy forearm and glanced at them in turn.

Mason moved closer to the muscular blacksmith and drew one of his weapons from its holster. He pushed the barrel into one of Carter's many chins and pulled back on its hammer. The outlaw glared into the unblinking eyes of the larger man.

'What you doing, friend?' Carter croaked.

'Where's our horse, old timer?' Mason snarled and jabbed the barrel into the throat of the liveryman. Carter took a step backwards but halted when he felt Snider's six-gun press into his backbone.

'You mean the palomino?' Carter asked as his mind raced for an answer that might not cost him his life.

Furiously, Mason sucked in air and gritted his teeth. He was so angry that every sinew in his body wanted him to squeeze his trigger, but he knew that by doing so would mean that they might never discover where the highly valuable stallion was. It took every scrap of his resolve, but the outlaw managed to control his urge to kill.

'Answer my damn question, mutton-head,' the horse thief repeated. 'Where's the horse? Where is our blasted horse? What you done with it?'

As terror surged through his large frame, Joe Carter knew that the gunmen were so unhinged by the discovery of the missing stallion that they might start shooting whatever he said. He took a deep breath.

'A young female took that horse with her when she headed out for Fort Liberty on her stagecoach,' the liveryman answered, expecting the gun at his throat to be fired at any moment.

A look of confusion filled the faces of both Snider and Mason as they absorbed Carter's words. The older of the horse thieves lowered his six-shooter from the throat of the blacksmith and stared into the glowing coals.

'A female?' Mason repeated as Snider moved around the large blacksmith to his partner's side.

Carter gave a nod. 'Yep. A darn vicious female. She scared the life out of me.'

Bren Mason shook his head in disbelief. 'You let her steal our horse? Why would a grown man allow a young female to do that?'

The blacksmith shrugged as he thought about how unlikely it sounded that someone of his size could be bettered by a tiny young female. But the truth was often less believable than tall tales.

'She had a Winchester and was willing to use it, friends,' Carter said as his eyes darted between both the horse thieves' drawn guns. 'She reckoned that the palomino belonged to her beloved. A critter called Iron Eyes, and she was set on taking that horse with her.'

Mason looked troubled by hearing the name of the famed bounty hunter, and said nothing for a few moments as his partner pressed up against the blacksmith.

'How'd she manage to do that?' Snider asked the large figure.

'That stallion was tied to the boot of her stagecoach on the tailgate,' Carter answered. 'She thundered out of here like a turkey with its tail feathers on fire.'

'And what is a female doing with a stagecoach?' Snider added as he turned to look at his partner. 'None of this makes any sense.'

'You're wrong, Jeb. It makes perfect sense,' Bren Mason had remained quiet since he had heard the liveryman spout the name of Iron Eyes. For a few moments his mind considered the familiar name, and then recalled the reputation of the notorious bounty hunter. A hombre he had never encountered but of whom he had heard many lurid tales. 'I've heard a lot of stories about this gal's beloved Iron Eyes. That varmint is the most dangerous bounty hunter ever to draw a breath.'

'I ain't ever heard of him,' Snider blinked hard.

'That's why you're still alive,' Mason sighed.

Carter looked at both outlaws in turn.

'If that horse belongs to Iron Eyes,' he stated. 'I'd not accept the animal as a gift.'

'She definitely said Iron Eyes?' the older of the outlaws questioned the large blacksmith. 'Are you sure?'

Carter nodded.

'Yep, that's the name she said,' he nodded. 'I didn't want to rile her up with her holding that Winchester. After all, I'm a real big target.'

Snider looked long and hard at his partner. 'You look kinda sickly, Bren. Why?'

Mason cleared his throat. He felt as though invisible hands were wrapped around his neck and throttling him as he recalled some of the stories he had heard about the notorious bounty hunter.

'Iron Eyes is deadly, Jeb.' He said quietly as a cold shiver ran down the length of his spine. 'The Injuns call him the ghost. They reckon he can't be killed 'coz he's already dead.'

Jeb Snider gave a grunting laugh.

'But he is dead, Bren,' he drawled. 'You know that, just like I know it. That bastard was dead up there in the mountains on the trail road. Dead as can be.'

A look of terror filled the whiskered face of the older horse thief as he stared blankly into the shimmering heat of the forge for a few moments.

'Now I ain't so sure,' Mason stammered.

'Quit fretting, Bren,' Snider laughed. 'We seen his dead carcass with our own eyes. Iron Eyes is dead. You know that, just like I know it.'

Mason turned and stared deep into the eyes of his partner for a few moments. His expression soon caused the younger outlaw to stop grinning.

'Is he?' Mason pushed past the blacksmith and stared out into the long street and towards the trail road that began its route through the multitude of trees. 'We never checked his body, Jeb boy. He just looked dead. By what I've heard of this critter, he never dies. Iron Eyes just never dies.'

'Are you serious?' Snider asked.

The blacksmith piped up.

'He's serious, right enough, young fella,' Carter told the outlaw as he sat down beside the forge. 'Look at his face. Your partner is deadly serious.'

Bren Mason turned and glared at the muscular blacksmith, then pointed at him.

'Saddle our horses, friend,' he snarled, before looking at his confused partner. 'Listen up. There's only one way we're gonna get our hands on that palomino, Jeb. We've gotta ride after that stagecoach and take it off that little lady.'

'By the sounds of it,' Snider gulped. 'She won't want to give up that horse without a fight.'

A devilish smile spread across the face of Bren Mason as he pondered the thought. He narrowed his eyes and began to nod eagerly to himself.

'Then we kill her, Jeb,' Mason said dryly. 'Simple as that.'

THIRTEEN

The words had barely left Bren Mason's mouth when his narrowed eyes observed the door to the sheriff's office open. His hand gripped the edge of the tall barb door and steadied it as he gazed through the diminishing light. The outlaw watched as Sheriff Casey Doyle stepped out into the dwindling light and turned up the collar of his coat to shield his neck against the evening breeze as it travelled along the length of the main street.

The horse thieves watched as Doyle closed the office door and locked it before starting his ritual walk around the logging town.

'Who is that critter, Bren?' Snider asked as he stood beside his partner. 'Whoever he is, he's mighty young.'

Mason knew only too well that age meant nothing if a man had a good six-gun and the ability to use it. He rubbed his unshaven jaw and exhaled heavily.

'He must be a sheriff or a deputy,' Mason reasoned. 'I caught sight of a glint of a tin star as he stepped out into the street.'

Two wagons suddenly appeared from a side street, swung on their axles and headed towards The Diamond Pin as well as the other saloons. The flatbeds of both vehicles were filled with burly loggers who had only one thing on their collective minds, and that was to enjoy themselves or die trying.

The street resounded to the sound of the eager loggers as they cheered their arrival at their favourite drinking holes. The wagon came to an abrupt halt outside the saloons in a cloud of dust. The burly loggers leapt from the flatbeds even before the vehicles had stopped. The large men charged noisily into the various saloons.

As clouds of dust from the wagon-wheel rims trailed across the wide street, Mason looked over his shoulder towards Joe Carter. The blacksmith had almost readied their pair of saddle horses in the centre of the large open space behind them. Mason returned his attention to the street.

As the dust cleared, the grisly outlaw noticed that there was no longer any sign of the sheriff. He tapped his partner's arm as his eyes vainly searched the street for the star packer.

'Where did that lawman go, Jeb?' he asked his companion with a nudge. 'Did you see where he went?'

Snider shrugged. 'Damned if I know where the varmint went, Bren. I was looking at them wagons pulling up outside them saloons. I didn't see where the lawman went.'

'Reckon it don't matter none,' Mason said thoughtfully. 'I doubt if that youngster will give any trouble.

We ain't wanted in this territory, so it's mighty doubtful he'll have any posters with our images on them. All we gotta do is ride up the trail road to where we left that Iron Eyes critter. The little gal should be there crying like a baby beside his busted body.'

'Then we steal the palomino back,' Snider grinned. 'Right?'

'Right,' Mason grinned, and then laughed. 'I doubt if she'll even notice us through her tears.'

The sweat-drenched Carter led the two saddle horses towards Snider and Mason. He held out the reins to the men and sighed heavily. The liveryman still did not know exactly what was happening, but he felt sure that the pair of heavily armed men were about to start something that neither he nor the rest of Bear Creek had ever experienced before.

'Here's your nags, gents,' the blacksmith said as he handed the long reins to both men. 'They're grained, watered and rested up and chomping on their bits.'

Without muttering a word, the older of the horse thieves fished a couple of silver coins from his vest pocket and flicked them into the huge hands of the blacksmith.

'Much obliged, gents,' Carter said as he dropped the coins into the pocket of his leather apron and backed away.

Mason was about to move around towards his mount's left stirrup when he caught sight of a nerve-shattering image. An image that shook him to the bone. The horse thief focused on the ghostly vision of the severely injured bounty hunter riding

135

along the trail road toward Bear Creek astride the prized palomino which he and his partner wanted more than anything.

It was a sight that stopped the outlaw in his tracks.

The outlaw stared open-mouthed at Iron Eyes as the gaunt figure guided the powerful palomino down the trail road into Bear Creek.

'Iron Eyes,' he muttered.

FOURTEEN

Jeb Snider stared in confusion at his fellow outlaw. He couldn't understand why Mason had stopped in his tracks before mounting his horse. He also did not understand why Mason had gone ashen.

'What's wrong, Bren?' Snider asked. 'You look like you seen a ghost.'

Mason gave a firm nod of his head. 'Maybe I have just seen a damn ghost. Look for yourself.'

He rushed to the tall barn doors and pointed at Iron Eyes cantering into the last throws of the setting sun upon the high-withered palomino stallion.

'Look, Jeb boy,' Mason stammered as his partner moved to his shoulder and stared out into the fading light at the unholy sight. 'Iron Eyes!'

The young outlaw stared at the chilling horseman, who looked more dead than alive as he sat astride the handsome horse. He gasped in a mixture of terror and bewilderment.

'It can't be,' Snider said before focusing upon the maimed features of the notorious bounty hunter. 'Or can it?'

Bren Mason suppressed his own trepidation and stared hard at the horrific horseman as Iron Eyes continued to ride into the heart of the logging town.

'It sure can, partner,' Mason hauled his six-shooter from its holster and jabbed at the air in the direction of the infamous bounty hunter. 'Somehow that stinking bastard didn't die up there in the forest like we figured. Don't ask me how, but he's still alive.'

'But he's dead, Bren,' the younger outlaw protested. 'We seen him dead up the trail road. He was covered in blood and was all busted up. That can't be Iron Eyes.'

Mason leaned against the tall barn door and stared long and hard at the younger outlaw.

'You name me another varmint that looks anything like that, Jeb,' he said as they watched the bounty hunter steer his palomino towards The Diamond Pin and dismount. 'Them tall tales about that critter might not be too far from the truth. Maybe he can't be killed like ordinary folks.'

Snider frowned as he heard his partner's words. Words which made no sense to the younger horse thief.

'Are you telling me that he's a ghost?' Snider asked as they watched the bounty hunter loop and secure his long reins to a hitching pole outside the saloon. 'He sure don't look like a ghost to me.'

'Me neither,' Mason admitted as he stared through the quickly fading light. 'But there he is, as ugly as the last time we set eyes upon him. Whatever he actually is, he has somehow managed to get his hands on that palomino again. I want that horse, Jeb boy.'

'You and me both,' Snider agreed.

'I intend getting it again,' Mason said in a hushed tone as he slid his six-gun back into its holster. 'Even if I have to kill every galoot in this town to do so, I'll get that mighty fine palomino again.'

'Yeah,' Snider sneered at the notion of killing. It was one of the few things he was actually good at. 'Nobody will stand in our way, Bren.'

Bren Mason focused on the tall lean bounty hunter as he stepped up on to the boardwalk outside The Diamond Pin. They watched as Iron Eyes paused for a moment and stood on the rim of the boardwalk studying the street carefully.

'That critter looks like he's ready to drop,' Snider noted as they carefully observed the gaunt bounty hunter. 'He ain't in no fit state to fend us off in a fight.'

'You might be right, Jeb boy,' Mason agreed. 'He sure looks fragile, and no mistake.'

Across the wide street, Iron Eyes pulled a cigar from his deep pockets and placed it between his razor-sharp teeth. The flickering light from a match that he ignited along a porch upright lit up the hideous features of the bounty hunter for a brief moment before its flame was blown out by the evening breeze. Iron Eyes filled his lungs with the strong smoke and savoured it for a few moments before exhaling.

Few creatures apart from the legendary bounty hunter had the ability to survive simply on cigars and

139

whiskey, but Iron Eyes had done so for half his existence. The breeze caught the tails of his long trail coat. As the coat swayed, the street echoed to the sound of the loose bullets in its pockets.

Mason and Snider felt their hearts pounding inside their chests as they observed the unholy Iron Eyes turn and enter the saloon in a cloud of cigar smoke.

'That sure is one ugly varmint, Jeb.'

'He sure is. How can Iron Eyes still be alive?' Snider stuttered in a disbelief that simply would not quit nagging at his guts. 'There are bodies in holes up on Boot Hill that look better than he does.'

The hardened features of Mason did not reply. He concentrated on the sight of the valuable stallion tethered to the hitching rail and began to drool.

'Dead or alive, he still ain't no wiser, Jeb boy,' Mason growled as he walked out into the street and began to home in on the palomino. 'Leaving that nag unprotected out there where anyone with half a brain can steal it. C'mon. Bring our saddle horses.'

Snider stared in alarm at his partner.

'What you going to do?' he croaked as he gathered up the reins of both their horses and started to lead them out from the livery stable after his companion.

Mason glanced over his wide shoulder.

'This is the perfect chance. I'm taking that palomino stallion, Jeb boy,' He stated. 'We'll be fifty miles away from here before that critter comes back out and notices his fancy horse is gone.'

'But what if he comes out and catches us?' the younger outlaw asked as he led their horses towards his partner. 'We don't know what we're dealing with here. What if them tall tales about Iron Eyes are right and he can't be killed? I don't fancy our chances fighting a critter that's already dead.'

Mason waved his arms in the air. 'You seen him standing on that boardwalk, Jeb. It was about all he could do to light his damn cigar. If that varmint tries to stop me, I'll surely kill him,'

'I guess so,' Snider was less confident. He had carved the wooden grips of both his six-shooters with notches to mark each of the folks that he had slain over the years, but Iron Eyes seemed different.

Very different.

Mason grunted. 'Quit fretting. I ain't gonna let anyone part us from that palomino again. I'm willing to kill even a dead man to keep my hands on that handsome animal.'

Jeb Snider hurriedly ran after his partner with the pair of horses in tow. The street grew darker with every beat of their hearts as they reduced the distance between the prized stallion and themselves.

'I don't like this,' Snider panted.

'Quit belly aching, Jeb,' Mason growled as they reached the hitching rail and stood less than a yard from the golden stallion. 'Look at this horse. It's gotta be worth a fortune to the right buyer. This ain't no cavalry nag, this is a thoroughbred, and as rare as gold dust in these parts.'

Snider held the saddle horses in check as his partner ran a gloved hand along the neck of the animal as he inspected it carefully. Snider knew that there was no possibility of changing the mind of the older horse thief.

'Hurry up, Bren,' he urged as he stepped into his stirrup and mounted his horse. 'Tie that horse to your saddle horn and let's ride out of here.'

With every word that spilled from his trembling lips, Snider kept looking anxiously at the swing doors of The Diamond Pin. He sensed that at any moment Iron Eyes could appear and start blasting his lethal Navy Colts at them.

'Quit dawdling, Bren,' Snider urged. 'We gotta get out of this damn town as fast as we can. We gotta put a lot of distance between that ugly varmint and ourselves.'

'Stop fretting,' Mason snarled. 'We got us plenty of time.'

The words did not calm the pounding heart of the anxious young outlaw as he gripped his reins and held his mount in check. Every bone in his body wanted to spur and ride away from the palomino stallion, but he knew that the valuable horse was worth a small fortune.

Greed outweighed the sands of wisdom.

Lamplight cascaded from the doors and windows of the saloons behind Mason's broad back as he pulled on the long reins and freed them from the hitching rail. The veteran thief stepped towards his own mount and carefully secured them to the saddle horn of his saddle.

The sturdy figure wrapped his reins around his wrist and stepped into his stirrup. As the confident

Mason hauled himself up on to his saddle, he grinned at his fretful partner and swung the horse around. But before he could mock his nervous companion he heard a loud noise from behind his back.

It was the distinctive sound of horses' hoofs pounding the ground as they pulled a speeding stagecoach behind them. Mason looked over his shoulder and stared in disbelief at the six-horse team thundering through the last of the day's sunshine down the trail road towards Bear Creek.

The vehicle rocked from side to side as its petite driver cracked a bullwhip above the heads of the galloping horses. It was travelling at breakneck pace.

'What the hell…?' Mason said.

'That must be the stagecoach the liveryman was telling us about, Bren,' Snider said as both he and his partner squinted through the clouds of dust at the unexpected sight.

Through the choking dust that kicked up from the team's hoofs and the coach's wheel rims, they could see Squirrel Sally quite clearly as she held the stagecoach's hefty reins in her tiny hands and steered her horses towards the startled horse thieves.

'That gal is plumb loco,' Mason screamed as he realized the fast-moving vehicle was on a collision course with them. The noise of chains battering against the long wooden traces filled the street.

Snider was frozen in absolute fear as he watched the advancing stagecoach bearing down upon them. He attempted to cry out to his partner, but no words managed to leave his mouth. His eyes widened as both he and Mason helplessly awaited the inevitable.

In the eerie twilight the snorting team of powerful black horses appeared like something escaping from the jaws of Hell itself. No mythical monsters could have appeared as daunting to the outlaws, who found themselves directly in the path of the stagecoach.

Mason attempted to steady his mount, but the palomino reared up behind him and kicked out viciously with its deadly hoofs at both horse and rider. The golden stallion's merciless hoofs hit the far smaller saddle horse and sent it stumbling forwards.

Snider watched helplessly as his partner was sent careering off his horse and crashed into the dust beneath the saloon boardwalk. The younger horseman held his mount in check as Mason staggered to his feet and vainly attempted to grab hold of his horse's loose reins and remount.

But that was impossible. A savage gash along the hindquarters of Mason's saddle horse had left the animal hobbling in agony.

Like a child calling to its parent for guidance, Snider croaked at his elder, but there was nothing either of them could do. There was no time.

No time to run. No time to think.

Mason nursed his aching bones as he limped between the horses and returned his mesmerized attention to the snorting team of horses that were thundering straight at them.

'Shoot them horses, Jeb,' Mason urged.

'I can't kill them all,' Snider replied as he held his skittish mount in check and fumbled for a six-gun.

'You can doggone try,' Mason snarled before dragging one of his .45s from its holster and firing at Squirrel Sally as she stared down through her fiery curls at them. With bullets passing within inches of her, she dropped down into the driver's box for cover.

Her six-horse team had been set on a course that no amount of lead could stop. They continued to thunder down the street towards the pair of horse thieves.

Mason and Snider stared in stunned horror as they watched the stagecoach hurtle towards them. The noise of the team's pounding hoofs echoing around the sturdy log cabins was unlike anything either of the horse thieves had ever heard before.

With bullets peppering the rim of the driver's box, Sally steered her galloping horses straight at the men beside the unmistakable palomino stallion. Even in the fading light, the fiery vixen had recognized both Snider and Mason as the men who had handed the stallion over to blacksmith Joe Carter outside the livery stable.

Sally knew that they had stolen the distinctive mount from her beloved Iron Eyes and left him to die up on the sun-baked trail road. She let out a whoop that was equal to anything that an Apache warrior might utter when attacking his enemies.

As far as the petite female was concerned, this was no different to the other battles she had become embroiled in since she had tagged along with the fearsome Iron Eyes.

This was war.

Her team of powerful black horses ploughed into the panicking horses. Snider was sent flying from his saddle by the impact, and landed at the feet of his partner.

Before either of the horse thieves could start firing their guns at the driver, Sally had grabbed her trusty Winchester and leapt like a puma from her high perch on to the sand. She crawled feverishly beneath the body of the coach as shots rang out from the outlaws' weaponry.

'Where'd that bitch go?' Mason raged.

'That driver was a woman?' Snider asked as he reloaded his smoking six-shooter. 'Are you sure?'

'I ain't ever seen a man with a chest like that, boy,' Mason snapped as they hid beside the still snorting palomino. 'Just try and kill her before she fills us with lead.'

The pair of startled horse thieves were using the mighty palomino as a shield from any return fire. Then suddenly they heard the sound of swing doors behind them.

Terrified that the infamous Iron Eyes had been alerted to trouble by the chaotic noise, Mason swung around and fanned his gun hammer in desperation at the saloon.

When the gunsmoke from his .45 cleared, Mason realized that he had made a mistake. A real big mistake: it wasn't the notorious bounty hunter who had stepped out from the relative safety of the saloons.

It was just curious loggers.

One by one the large men had been hit by the reckless shots and fallen like trees across the boardwalk. Lamplight from within The Diamond Pin spilled over the human wreckage and highlighted the scarlet blood that ran freely from their wounds.

Only when streams of blood trickled over the lip of the boardwalk did Mason realize his mistake. He switched his weapons quickly and cocked the hammer of a fresh .45. Without missing a beat, he resumed blasting over the ornate Mexican saddle at the stagecoach.

Bullets ricocheted off the body of the stagecoach as Squirrel Sally crawled unseen [from behind it and then] under the closest of the wagons. The sound of her cranking the mechanism of her rifle was drowned out by the constant gunfire coming from behind the trio of horses close to the boardwalk.

Just like the horse thieves, Sally could not see a clear target to fire at. She gripped the rifle tightly and decided to risk everything by getting even closer to the outlaws.

Sally stared through the legs of the wagon team at the familiar legs of the palomino stallion. The problem was that the constant gunfire was making the horses nervous. Their mighty legs were stomping the ground and crushing it beneath their hoofs.

She was about to start crawling when she saw a long thin shadow trace a path from the saloon swing doors to where she lay on her belly [under the wagon].

Squirrel Sally immediately recognized the pathetically thin shadow and beamed.

'Iron Eyes.' Sally whispered.

FIFTEEN

The Diamond Pin's swing doors continued rocking on their hinges but went unnoticed and unheard behind the bounty hunter's wide back. As clouds of gunsmoke drifted across the front of the blood-splattered saloon the brutally maimed Iron Eyes observed the horrific scene with cold-blooded indifference. The unblinking bounty hunter sucked the last of the smoke from the well-chewed cigar, and then dropped it on to the boardwalk between the bodies of the lifeless loggers piled at his feet.

The fleshly spilled blood extinguished the mangled cigar quickly. A pitiful hiss and a curl of smoke went undetected as the horse thieves continued to shoot blindly at the stationary stagecoach in the desperate bid to kill the fearless Sally.

Iron Eyes moved silently like a big cat across the blood-stained boardwalk to its very edge. He paused and stared through his matted mane of long black hair in the direction of the two outlaws as they continued to fire their arsenal of weaponry at the already bullet-riddled stagecoach.

The bounty hunter noted that Mason and Snider were secreted just beyond his palomino stallion, which itself was close to the heads of the loggers' two-horse wagon team.

Like a ravenous vulture, the bounty hunter watched his prey.

Then without a single thought for his own safety, the bounty hunter stepped on to the top of the hitching rail and propelled his battered frame on to the loggers' empty flatbed. No cougar could have matched his agility as his mule-eared boots landed on the boards and he dropped to his knees. Iron Eyes crouched as his skeletal hands dragged both his Navy Colts from his deep trail-coat pockets.

His bony thumbs pulled back on his gun hammers until the matched pair of lethal six-shooters were fully cocked and ready to deliver their own brand of justice.

The relentless firing continued unabated. Each shot echoed around the small settlement like thunderclaps, and Iron Eyes knew that there was only one sure way to end this devilish onslaught.

For a brief moment his unblinking eyes darted from the back of the wagon flatbed to the battered stagecoach as chunks of it were severed from its body. He wondered where the tempestuous Squirrel Sally had gone, and that troubled him. A multitude of questions flashed through his mind, but mainly he wondered where she had gone.

It seemed impossible that she could have survived such an unending barrage of bullets, but if anyone could, Squirrel could.

Iron Eyes stared through the limp strands of black hair that masked his uncanny features from uninvited prying attention, and kept watching the outlaws.

They were trapped, he thought. Trapped like the vermin they were. He was about to rise when he heard running coming from behind him. Iron Eyes turned his head and watched Casey Doyle running feverishly towards the stagecoach.

Iron Eyes could see the glinting tin star pinned to the young lawman's coat. He raised one of his trusty weapons and squeezed its trigger. A flame blasted from the gun barrel through a circle of smoke.

Sheriff Doyle came to an abrupt halt when the bullet hit the ground before his large boots and showered debris over him. The lawman looked up and saw the shadowy bounty hunter holding the smoking six-gun in his thin hand.

As Doyle drew his own weapon from its holster, he saw Iron Eyes gesturing for him to take cover. The confused young sheriff had been drawn toward the constant gunfire like a moth to an unguarded flame. Then he saw the terrifying bounty hunter on the flatbed.

'Take cover!' Iron Eyes shouted at the startled lawman. 'You'll surely die if you take another step.'

Doyle heeded the advice and moved to the side of the other wagon. His mind raced as he listened to the deafening crescendo of gunfire. A million splinters floated in the darkening air as bullets continued to hit the stationary stagecoach.

Iron Eyes mustered his flagging energy as he stared through the clouds of gunsmoke at the desperate horse thieves. Both gunmen were terrified, he thought. They were firing their weaponry as if trying to fend off an invisible enemy.

The bounty hunter raised his lean frame up in readiness to sprint forwards as Jeb Snider finally managed to remount his skittish horse. Iron Eyes hesitated as he watched the outlaw trying to get control of his feisty mount.

Iron Eyes raised one of his Navy Colts and carefully aimed it the younger of the outlaws. It was obvious that Snider was about to flee the brutal bloodbath. The bounty hunter knew that he would have to fire quickly if he were to have any chance of killing one of the outlaws.

Then just as he was about to squeeze his trigger, a deafening shot came from somewhere. The shot was lethally accurate and found its target. In astonishment Iron Eyes watched as Snider buckled on his saddle. Then a second shot carved through the shadows and also located its mark.

The horse thief fell from his bucking mount like a rag doll being tossed from a crib. His lifeless body rolled across the sand as Mason attempted to grab the horse's bridle before it galloped away from the mayhem.

With his icy stare glued to the desperate outlaw as he attempted to control the wide-eyed horse, Iron Eyes rammed his Navy Colts into his deep pockets and flexed his talon-like hands in anticipation of the impending duel.

The bounty hunter sprang into action.

Defying his pain, Iron Eyes ran forwards, leapt on to the driver's seat and then stepped on to the broad back of one of the wagon's horses. With his long black hair trailing behind his scrawny carcass, Iron Eyes vaulted over his palomino stallion towards Mason. He spread out his long arms as far as they would stretch and caught Mason around the neck as he headed towards the churned-up ground. The outlaw felt himself being dragged off his feet by the sheer force of being tackled around his neck by the bounty hunter's outstretched claw.

The force of the impact caused Mason to fire his gun wildly before both men hit the ground and somersaulted into the outlaw's badly injured horse. They scrambled apart as Iron Eyes threw his emaciated frame to the side as Mason unleashed another deafening shot.

The shot lifted the loose fabric of Iron Eyes' already torn and tattered trail coat away from his pitifully thin frame. But as Mason went to cock his .45 again, the sound of another weapon being discharged filled the confines of the murky area and caused the horse thief to jerk back as a bullet hit him dead centre.

A pained expression on Mason's face was highlighted by the lamplight that spilled from the saloon and cascaded over both adversaries. Iron Eyes got to his feet and stared at Mason in equal confusion. Both men wondered where the shot had come from as Iron Eyes' infamous six-shooters were still in his coat pockets.

Mason felt his gun slip from his fingers and drop to the sandy ground. Then as more blood spread across his shirt front, his watery eyes looked at the bounty hunter.

'So you're Iron Eyes?' Mason croaked as blood trickled from the corner of his mouth. Then his entire body shuddered and he fell on to his knees.

'Yep,' Iron Eyes gave a nod. 'And you and your dead pal tried to kill me to get your stinking hands on my horse.'

Mason grabbed his chest in a vain effort to stem the flow of blood. He spat a crimson lump of goo at the tall bounty hunter and grinned.

'And just how did someone like you ever manage to lay their hands on a fine thoroughbred stallion like that beauty?' he asked as blood trailed from his mouth. 'Tell me that. How did you come to own such a fine hunk of horseflesh?'

Iron Eyes squinted hard.

'I killed the vaquero that was riding it,' he recalled.

Mason gave out a loud guttural laugh. Then another shot rang out and ended the horse thief's hilarity. The shot was as deadly accurate as the first and hit Mason a mere inch from the first in the centre of his chest.

As the smoke cleared, Iron Eyes could see the lifeless body of Bren Mason lying on his back staring with dead eyes up at the heavens.

His attention was then drawn to the smoking barrel of a Winchester as it appeared from between the legs of his golden stallion. Squirrel Sally was holding the trusty weapon as she clambered to her feet.

Sally beamed at the tall bounty hunter, totally unaware that her perfectly formed body had once again escaped the restrictions of her trail-worn clothing.

'Ain't you pleased to see me, darling?' she asked.

'I guess so,' observed Iron Eyes as he pulled a cigar from his pocket and then placed it between his teeth, staring at the dead outlaws as he calculated their collective worth. As he struck a match with a thumbnail he watched Sally lift her rifle to her lips and kiss it.

'I killed them both, darling.' She grinned. 'I done it for you. Ain't you pleased?'

Iron Eyes blew smoke at the bodies. 'I'm pleased.'

Sally clapped her hands together and began hopping up and down as she moved around the emaciated bounty hunter. Finally she stopped and looked up into his savaged features.

'Should I book us a room at the hotel, beloved?' she cooed at the emotionless face. 'We could get into bed and snuggle up together and see what happens. What do you reckon?'

'Why?' he drawled through smoke.

She nearly blushed. 'You know why, sweetheart.'

Iron Eyes frowned and filled his lungs with cigar smoke again as he thought about her proposal.

'I saved your life, didn't I?' she smugly smiled. 'I figure you owe me something for that. We are betrothed, after all. It's time you done something to prove you love me as much as I love you.'

Iron Eyes exhaled smoke into her face.

'You trouble me, Squirrel.'

FINALE

Doc Parry was bruised and bleeding as he finally found the strength to open the stagecoach door and slide from the bullet-riddled vehicle. He stared through blurred eyes at the sight of the dead outlaws, and then looked at the two very different people who were simply staring at one another. As he sat on the step of the coach he heard Sheriff Casey Doyle cautiously appear beside him from the shadows.

'What in tarnation has been going on here, Doc?' he asked before holstering his .45.

Doc Parry shrugged. 'Damned if I know, Sheriff. I just spent the last hour or so bouncing around inside this stagecoach. The ground is still shaking under my shoes.'

Doyle looked at the perilous pair and rubbed the nape of his neck thoughtfully. He leaned closer to the medical man.

'Do you reckon I ought to arrest someone, Doc?' he asked innocently. 'It sure seems like I should arrest someone.'

Doc Parry shook his head and stared at the confused lawman standing at his side. 'I'd not try to arrest either of them folks, if I was you, Casey. That little gal has a mighty bad temper. Who knows what she might do?'

'Yeah, I tangled with her last night,' Doyle recalled before shuddering. 'She don't pull her punches.'

Iron Eyes had silently studied the faces of both Mason and Snider against the crumpled wanted posters he carried in his deep pockets before moving to the side of the female. He attempted to cover up her exposed breasts with the remains of her shirt and then gave up.

'I know what you're thinking,' Sally sighed heavily. 'You wanna play with my chests. Right?'

'Nope,' he argued before turning away. 'I was thinking you need new trail gear, Squirrel. Them threads sure ain't cutting the mustard.'

She stomped her foot. 'Saving your worthless hide has kinda taken its toll on them.'

'These varmints ain't wanted here but they got prices on their heads in Arizona, Squirrel,' he said through a cloud of cigar smoke. 'If we transport them over the state line, we can make a lot of money.'

Sally's eyes narrowed as she frowned at the bounty hunter.

'And exactly how do we take their bodies over the border, Iron Eyes?' she asked. 'How do we do that?'

The question had only just left her lips when she saw the bounty hunter staring at her stagecoach thoughtfully. She then knew what he intended.

'Are you figuring on using my stagecoach to move them stinking corpses, beloved?' she snorted. 'The last time you done that my damn stage stank of death for months.'

His bullet-coloured eyes looked at her.

'But these corpses are fresh,' Iron Eyes tilted his head and reasoned. 'If you drive fast, they won't have time to start smelling, Squirrel.'

Sally exhaled. 'Who gets the reward money?'

'I figured we could share it,' Iron Eyes replied. 'Half each sounds about right.'

Sally considered the proposal for few seemingly endless moments as they both moved to the stage-coach. Both Doc Parry and Sheriff Doyle were hurriedly heading down the smoke filled street. Sally caught a brief glimpse of the medical man and sighed heavily.

'I done forgot about the Doc being inside the coach,' she mumbled to herself as Iron Eyes reached her side. She fluttered her eyelashes at her tall companion. 'I should get more than just half. I shot the critters, after all.'

Iron Eyes reached inside the body of the coach and pulled a bottle from a busted box. He stared at the amber liquor and reluctantly nodded.

'Okay, you can have it all, Squirrel,' he said before pulling the cork from the neck of the bottle and spitting it at the bodies.

Sally skipped around him in triumphant joy.

'I bested you, Iron Eyes,' she laughed out loud. 'I done bested you.'

Iron Eyes took a swig of the fearsome whiskey and stared at her as its fumes filled his pain-racked frame. There wasn't a hint of emotion in his heavily scarred face. He was just relieved that once again he had managed to delay sharing a hotel room with the overly excited young female.

'You trouble me, Squirrel,' he sighed before returning the cigar to his mouth. 'You plumb trouble me.'

THE END